PROTECTING

the Cittern

PROTECTING
the Cittern

JOHN CAMMALLERI

iUniverse, Inc.
New York   Bloomington

Protecting the Cittern

This is a work of fiction. All of the characters, names, incidents, organizations, and dialogue in this novel are either the products of the author's imagination or are used fictitiously.

iUniverse books may be ordered through booksellers or by contacting:

iUniverse
1663 Liberty Drive
Bloomington, IN 47403
www.iuniverse.com
1-800-Authors (1-800-288-4677)

Because of the dynamic nature of the Internet, any Web addresses or links contained in this book may have changed since publication and may no longer be valid. The views expressed in this work are solely those of the author and do not necessarily reflect the views of the publisher, and the publisher hereby disclaims any responsibility for them.

ISBN: 978-1-4502-4220-2 (sc)
ISBN: 978-1-4502-4222-6 (dj)
ISBN: 978-1-4502-4221-9 (ebook)

Printed in the United States of America

iUniverse rev. date: 07/14/2010

To Evelyn

Acknowledgments

I'd like to thank my wife, Evelyn, who read every word of every revision and gave me wonderful feedback and a few key plot points. I am grateful to my good friend Ginger Pona, R.N., who provided valuable input regarding the medical references. Special thanks go to all the members of the Morningside Library Writers' Workshop in Port St. Lucie, Florida, who helped me immeasurably in guiding me through the writing process and gave me extremely valuable critiques; I learned a lot from them. Lastly, I appreciate all the help from George Nedeff and the editorial staff at iUniverse, who provided many suggestions that were critical in getting this book into its final form.

Chapter I

December 2003

*G*LANCING UP AT the sky, I wiped the dirt from my hands and then stepped back to stand with the rest of my family as we waited for the funeral service to end. The forecast had called for snow, and it felt like it would start any minute. The clouds looked heavy, and I folded my arms to ward off the chill.

Throwing a handful of soil on top of the casket seemed like a meaningless gesture, just like anything else based on superstition. The act meant nothing to me, nor did the rest of the proceedings—I was simply going through the motions. As I glanced at my watch every few minutes, my mind wandered from one random thought to the next: the work that was waiting on my desk; how the Giants would do on Sunday; if I'd be able to fix my slice when golf season started up. Everything was more important than what was happening in front of me.

I remained completely detached as the service ended and we all walked away from the gravesite. Despite everything that had happened between us over the years, I thought I should feel a deeper sense of loss; but I didn't, and I couldn't force myself to feel any differently. I wondered how many other sons were completely apathetic after putting their fathers in the ground.

If anyone noticed how unmoved I was, they may have believed

1

I was being strong for the family—behaving like a man. It didn't matter to me what they thought. I glanced back at the grave where my father now lay. It was in a relatively new section of Holy Cross Cemetery, with only a few other graves nearby. *Perfect for my father,* I thought. *Fewer people to annoy him.*

I climbed into the limousine with my wife, our daughter, and my newly widowed mother. Kathy and I had been through a lot since we met nearly thirty years earlier, and I was always amazed that she married me after getting to know my father. Perhaps she didn't see much of him in me. At fifty, Kathy was still as radiant as the day we'd met. Her soft brown hair and blue eyes stirred me as much as ever. We'd faced many challenges and difficulties over the years, but our marriage had gotten stronger as we worked through them.

Twenty-three years old and a graduate student at Princeton's Woodrow Wilson School, Lisa was one semester away from earning her master's degree in public affairs. She was as smart as she was beautiful, with, thankfully, most of Kathy's features rather than mine.

My mother, Clara, short, thin, and slightly stooped over, showed every one of her eighty-one years in her silver hair and wizened face.

The driver started the engine, preparing to take us back to DeAngelo's Funeral Home. From there we transferred to our four-year-old Ford Taurus and drove to Ernesto's Restaurant, where lunch would be served. My mother didn't want people coming to the house, bringing endless casseroles that would eventually be thrown out, so she and I agreed to host something simple. I wasn't expecting too many people to join us; attendance at the church service was low, and fewer people were at the cemetery. The people who showed up came to support my mother rather than to mourn for my father, although in actuality she was holding up very well.

*   *   *   *

A week earlier I was alone with my father in his room at Tranquil Meadows, the long-term care facility where he spent his last few months, when he finally passed on. Kathy and I had just left him after a brief visit; when we got home, she realized she had forgotten her purse in his room. I returned alone to get it and ended up watching him die. I then brought my mother to the nursing home to see him and make the necessary arrangements.

My mother looked at my father for a few minutes, lying lifeless in his bed. She cried very briefly and then just stared at him, sighing. I suppose there was a touch of genuine sadness—they'd been married for over fifty years—but I'm sure she mostly felt relief that a load had finally been lifted from her shoulders. She had endured many years of verbal, mental, and physical abuse at his hands, and watching his steady decline since he was first hospitalized thoroughly wore her out.

Standing at the foot of his bed, she spoke to his corpse, as if he could really hear her. "I hope you find happiness now, Sammy. Nothing ever made you happy. Now you'll be with Anna in heaven." My sister died much too young many years before after a battle with leukemia, and my mother was grieving more for her after twenty-five years than for my father after less than an hour.

Under different circumstances, I would have challenged her belief in heaven and other fantasies, but I held back my comments. I don't believe in an afterlife, although if there were one, I always felt he would be going in the other direction; and if people were able to reunite in death, Anna would have chosen to avoid him altogether. She had as many issues with him as I did. Regardless of what really happens after death, I knew we were all going to be happier without him.

*   *   *   *

We pulled into the parking lot at Ernesto's, a typical family-style Italian restaurant with two rooms in the back for private affairs. The cold wind of the gray, mid-December day gusted up, and light snow fell as I helped my mother out of the front seat; Kathy and Lisa emerged from the back. I took my wife's hand and Lisa took her grandmother by the arm as we approached the entrance. We made our way to one of the rooms in the back, passing the collection of faux-marble statues that lined the hallway. A few people were already waiting inside, and the rest would arrive shortly. Aunt Luisa saw us entering and immediately walked over to greet us, leaving a friend of the family in mid-sentence, her mouth agape.

Aunt Luisa was the widow of my father's oldest brother, Paulie. At eighty-six, she was as energetic, bombastic, and overdramatic as ever. She put her arms around my mother and squeezed. "Oh, Clara, you're going to be okay," she said, kissing the air on both sides of her cheeks. "It took me a while after I lost Paulie, but you learn to adjust."

Paulie and my father were cut from the same mold. They were very pleasant when they had to be, mostly to people outside their immediate families, either because it made them look good or it suited them for business purposes. But to their wives, children, or people they didn't have any use for, they were demanding, abusive, and impossible to please. The middle brother, Frank, was the same. From what I could piece together from some vague family stories, they had either inherited or learned this behavior from their father, my grandfather Enzo.

Aunt Luisa was left pretty well off when she sold Uncle Paulie's Italian provisions business soon after he died, and her life was never better. For my father's funeral, she dressed as if she were going to opening night at the Metropolitan Opera. She wore a stylish black beaded dress, beautifully contrasted by a large string of pearls around her neck. A three-carat diamond ring graced the finger where her wedding band had been, and a tennis bracelet on her right wrist begged to be noticed. Her rouge and lipstick were red and thick, and her hair was done up and sprayed until it was as stiff as a medieval helmet. But then, Aunt Luisa had always been conscious of her appearance, even before Uncle Paulie died.

My aunt stood in stark contrast to my mother, who dressed as simply as possible. Mom never fussed with her appearance, mostly because of her Depression-era sense of frugality, which had been reinforced by my father's penny-pinching ways. However, in this case, she looked appropriate. She wore a plain black dress and a black headscarf to cover her short hair. She wore no makeup and no jewelry except for her wedding ring and a wristwatch. The watch had belonged to Anna, and my mother had worn it since shortly after Anna's death.

"Thank you, Lu," my mother said. "I know. Tony's been a big support, and he'll help me with everything I need."

"You take care of your mother, Tony," Aunt Luisa said, looking straight at me, almost as though she were presenting a challenge.

"Don't worry, Aunt Lu. She'll be fine."

Kathy gave me a gentle nudge, indicating that it was time to enter the room where lunch would be served. It looked like everyone was there. I took my mother by the elbow. "Time to sit down, Ma."

We walked in and sat at a table that included Aunt Luisa; her son, Vincent; and her daughter-in-law, Donna. Unsurprisingly, Aunt Luisa's daughter, Candace, and son-in-law, Angelo, hadn't bothered flying in from Tampa. Frank and his wife, Julia, were deceased, and their two children remained at home in California and Arizona with their spouses. I guess my cousins felt they'd rather stay in the warm weather than come to New Jersey in December.

It was awkward seeing Vince and Donna, and I was sure the feeling was mutual. After years of estrangement, we exchanged nothing but stilted conversation. It was obvious they were there out of necessity, not love. I was actually glad my out-of-state cousins had chosen not to attend. My father and his brothers hadn't been close, and, as a consequence, neither were their children. I never heard any explanation as to why my father and uncles had fallen out, but I'd also never been curious enough to ask.

I watched as the rest of the attendees took their seats, talking and laughing. I couldn't help thinking that they'd all just come for the free meal. I gave a quick nod to acknowledge some past and current neighbors and saw a few of my mother's old friends. Noticeably absent from both the funeral and the luncheon were the barbers who had worked in my father's shop or whom he knew from the union, or any of his so-called friends from his Friday-night poker games. The barbers knew him too well, and his poker cohorts were just happy to take his money.

The wait staff was soon serving a standard Italian meal of salad, ziti, and chicken parmigiana, with a lemon cake for dessert. Bottles of cola and Chianti were placed at each table on the cliché red-and-white-checked tablecloths. Throughout the meal, almost everyone walked up to my mother and me to express their condolences and offer to do whatever she needed—the usual empty words one says at a time like this. One by one they came to our table, shook my hand, and kissed my mother. "Sorry for your loss" was the quote of the day. I've said those same words myself many times and could tell when they were sincere or mechanical; I've been on both sides of that fence.

As I was finishing my cake, Kathy leaned over and whispered in my ear, "I think you should say a few words; people will be leaving soon. No one said anything at the service." I gave her a pained expression, but she just smiled and nodded in encouragement. "Try to say something nice."

She was right, as usual, but I hadn't given much thought to saying anything. The standard advice to speak from the heart definitely wouldn't apply, but I had to say something, if only for appearance's sake. Sadly, my father had kept so much to himself over the years that what I knew of him was only what he wanted to reveal to us, and that wasn't always pleasant. It suddenly occurred to me that I wished I'd known him better. I slowly rose, clearing my throat.

"Could I have everyone's attention, please?" I said, lightly tapping on my water glass. The chatter in the room slowly died down. It gave me a little more time to think.

Speaking haltingly, I gave it my best shot. "First, on behalf of my mother and the whole Giordano family, I want to thank everyone for the kindness and support you have given her the last few days, and throughout my father's illness, and for paying your respects here today. Even though he had been in declining health for several months, the end still came unexpectedly. Many of you have known my father for years, and I'm sure you have some special memories of him. As his son, I know he was a hard worker, built a successful business, and always managed to make sure we had what we needed.

"One of my most vivid memories of him is how much he loved music. His hands were always waving in the air, conducting the orchestra, whenever a symphony or opera played on his stereo. And he was always plucking and strumming his cittern. He hated when I called it a guitar. I never saw him treat anything else with such respect. No one else was allowed to touch it. He always seemed at peace with his music.

"It's going to be very different not having him around, but I'm sure that, in time, we will adjust. Mom and the rest of us will do our best to get through the next few days and weeks. Thanks again."

As I sat down, Kathy gave me an "atta boy" pat on the back. I leaned toward her. "At least I thought of something nice to say."

Looking from table to table, I sensed that everyone felt I was just going through the motions. They were right, and for the first time I regretted the intensity of my feelings toward him. I thought it was too late to ever really know my father.

Chapter 2
Christmas 1957

CHRISTMAS IN THE Giordano household
was like every other holiday or family
occasion—extremely stressful. Anna and Tony could sense the
tension even as young as they were in 1957. Anna was the eldest
at seven, and Tony was five, and they formed a close bond early
on. Beyond the usual sibling arguments they were involved in as
children, there was always something stronger that drew them
together and strengthened their alliance—fear of their father.

Clara was in the kitchen with her mother, Assunta, whom Anna
and Tony called Nana'Sunta. At fifty-four, Assunta was slightly
stocky, with long, salt-and-pepper hair rolled up in a bun. The
women worked in silence, occasionally humming an old Italian
tune. There was no need to communicate. They'd worked together
in the kitchen so many times before; they knew what needed to be
done. They maneuvered around the kitchen, gathering utensils and
ingredients, do-si-doing around each other like a championship
dance team at a hoedown. Assunta was kneading the dough for the
ravioli that would become the first course for dinner. Clara had the
tomato sauce simmering on the stove and was making the filling for
the stuffed artichokes. The roast was already prepared, waiting to
go in the oven when the time was right.

Clara's father, Bruno, walked into the kitchen and inhaled deeply over the pot of sauce. He was short at five-foot-six, with wispy gray hair and a joking personality.

"Smells-a real good. When-a do we eat?"

"You've got a long wait, Pa. Don't worry, we'll call you. Go play with the kids."

Bruno left to find his grandchildren.

"Dov'è Savino?" Assunta asked, using Sammy's given name. She switched frequently from Italian to broken English, many times within the same sentence.

"In the den, watching TV."

"I'm-a no surprise. He all the time avoid *la famiglia*. You father, he no like-a this."

"Ma, you know how hard Sammy works. When he gets some time off, he likes to relax." Clara always made excuses, even though Sammy's reclusiveness bothered her, too. It caused a lot of friction within the family and limited her ability to form any strong friendships. On more than one occasion, a conversation she had with the mother of one of Tony or Anna's friends would lead to a dinner invitation. Inevitably there would be either an abrupt cancellation of plans or a very uncomfortable evening. Eventually, Clara stopped trying.

Sammy had a successful barbershop in the Newark suburb of Belleville, where they lived in a duplex owned by Bruno and Assunta, paying a modest rent. Each side of the house was a mirror image of the other, with two bedrooms, a kitchen, a living room, and a dining room. A small foyer at the common entrance in the front of the house separated the two sides. The doors from the foyer into each living room were often left open, making the two sides feel like a single big house. Each side had a private entrance in the back that accessed the kitchen from a small, enclosed porch. With only one spare bedroom on each side, Tony slept in his parents' half of the house, and Anna used her grandparents' spare room. A basement spanned the entire length of the house. Sammy's den was added in a corner of the basement shortly after they moved in, at his own expense, when he decided he needed a place to get away.

In spite of the comfortable living conditions and convenience to his barbershop, Sammy hated living there. After years of working hard to develop his business, he was able to afford a home of his own. But when Bruno and Assunta built this house, Sammy was just starting out, and it made financial sense to move in with them. What he didn't realize at the time was that Clara's emotional bond to her mother was so strong that moving out would never be a realistic option. Growing up, Clara had never shown any attempt at independence or rebellion toward her parents. She was always shy and kept to herself, and she had few friends.

Another reason they stayed was the kids. "It's time we found our own house," Sammy said shortly after Tony was born, trying to have an intelligent conversation about the possibility.

"Where?" Clara replied. "Anna and Tony are a handful. Ma is a big help to me with them. And my parents need me to get around since they don't drive. I'd have to come from our house to pick them up. Everything's so much easier the way it is. We don't need to change anything."

Sammy, recognizing Clara's inability to function without her mother, gave up his desire to move and gradually estranged himself from Clara and her parents. At family functions, he was aloof; when there were events at the house, he hid in his den with the door shut, unavailable to everyone. He would stay there and brood over the prospect of another holiday with the people he despised.

*   *   *   *

Earlier in the day, Anna and Tony excitedly ran into the living room in the front of the house. There, the Christmas tree waited, covered with garland, tinsel, and brightly colored balls, with presents piled underneath. During the rest of the year, both Sammy and Clara were extremely frugal with themselves and the children; they didn't spend a dime unless it was absolutely necessary, such as new clothes for the beginning of the school year. Unnecessary treats were frowned upon, and the children learned very early not to ask for candy or a comic book. But for Christmas, Clara indulged Anna and Tony, at least by her standards. They each received two or three of the popular boys' and girls' toys from that year, a few books, and some play clothes. Sammy was never part of this process.

He told Clara to buy what she wanted for them but not to overdo it. Somehow she managed to stay within the unspecified limits he set.

The gifts under the tree that year included a Betsy Wetsy doll and a record player with some children's records for Anna, while Tony received a Mickey Mouse guitar and a Roy Rogers gun and holster. The children also got assorted clothes and books that they looked at quickly but set back down in favor of the new playthings.

Clara bought the guitar because Tony had gotten in trouble several times for sneaking into Sammy's den to play with the cittern, and she hoped this would satisfy his desire to play an instrument. Tony should have known better, but his curiosity always got the better of him. Sammy eventually bought a small curio cabinet, in which he kept his prized possession under lock and key.

*   *   *   *

Clara and Assunta started working early in the morning to prepare dinner, as they did for every holiday. Sammy never offered help of any kind, either with preparation or cleanup, but then neither did Bruno; they believed kitchen work was women's work. Children were not part of that logic, so Anna and Tony were asked to help set the table, which they did reluctantly.

With Christmas dinner finally prepared, Clara descended the stairs to the basement, knocked on the door to Sammy's den, closed her eyes in anticipation, and slowly let herself in.

"Dinner's ready, Sammy." As she entered the room, she knew what to expect, but she always cringed. Clara would never send one of the kids to get him; she knew what they'd see.

He was lying on the sofa, eyes closed, his cittern cradled in his arms. A sleeveless T-shirt covered his wiry frame. The television provided the only light as it flickered the images of a choir singing Christmas carols. Smoke and a stale odor permeated the room. An ashtray filled with cigarette butts sat on the coffee table in front of the sofa. Another half-smoked cigarette dangled loosely between his lips. Sammy grunted in acknowledgment and crushed it out.

He rose and put on his shirt, which was draped over the arm of the sofa. Then he grudgingly walked out of his fortress.

Sammy, Clara, and the children sat at the table with Assunta and Bruno. Sammy's parents, Enzo and Rosa, were with Paul and Luisa in Ridgewood; they alternated where they went each year. Sammy and his brothers, never close, grew further apart the older they got, and they mostly saw one another at weddings and funerals. There was never a holiday that the entire Giordano clan celebrated together. Besides the brothers' strained relationship, none of the wives wanted to take on dinner preparations for all three families, nor did they want their houses packed with people. So the Giordano brothers spent the holidays with only their immediate families. They never even picked up the telephone to wish one another a merry Christmas.

Strained conversation occasionally broke the silence at the dinner table. Bruno, always jovial and a favorite of the kids, asked, "So, did-a Santa treat you two good this-a year?"

The children replied, "Yes," in unison as they glanced at their father. Anna and Tony were both fearful that they might be speaking out of turn. But Sammy's attention was focused on his plate.

"I like my guitar; it's got Mickey on it," Tony said, feeling bold. "It's nicer than Daddy's."

Sammy looked up and directed his attention at Tony. The stare was all that was needed. "I know," Tony added, "it's not a guitar. I'm sorry."

Clara and her parents discussed some relatives and the prospect of visiting a few before New Year's. Sammy gave her a quick look that clearly meant she should exclude him from any visiting, but Clara knew very well not to ask him to join them.

The children couldn't wait to be excused so they could go back to their new toys, but they knew better than to ask. They both kept shifting in their seats, moving the food on their plates with their forks. Tony put his elbows on the table and leaned his chin in the palms of his hands, closing his eyes.

"Tony, sit up straight," Clara said.

Tony jumped in his seat and put his hands in his lap, looking at his mother with an impish smile.

When the adults had had their last sip of espresso and the children had finished their cake and milk, they were allowed to leave the table and play. Sammy retreated to his den to take his usual after–dinner nap.

It wasn't long before Anna and Tony got overexcited playing. Tony did an Elvis Presley impersonation, strumming on his Mickey Mouse guitar and jumping up and down. In his den, Sammy turned over on his couch, unable to fall asleep. The constant noise irritated him. Eventually, Tony's loud, off-key singing, the vibrations from the jumping, and Anna's laughter were too much for Sammy. There was no sleeping with that racket going on upstairs. He yanked open the door to his den. Slamming his feet on every step, he stormed up the stairs and went into the living room.

"Don't you imbeciles know I'm trying to sleep?" he yelled.

Anna and Tony stopped in their tracks. Clara and her parents listened from the dining room, where they were still engaged in conversation.

Sammy pointed at the floor directly in front of him.

"Come over here now! Both of you!"

The children froze. Anna's lower lip quivered, and her eyes watered up.

"I said, 'Come here.'" Sammy pointed at the floor again, his voice growing louder.

Tony put down his guitar, and they both slowly walked toward their father, holding each other's hands. They could barely place one foot in front of the other as they inched toward him. Their faces were frozen as they registered their father's anger.

"Now!" Sammy yelled at the top of his voice. A water stain grew on the front of Tony's pants. Clara, Assunta, and Bruno rose from the dining room table.

The children reached the spot where Sammy was pointing, standing side by side. Clara and her parents entered the living room just as Sammy put his hands on the sides of their heads and banged them together.

"Now, shut up and let me sleep."

The children ran crying to Assunta, who wrapped her arms around them. Sammy walked back to his den. He knew they were glaring at him, and he didn't care. What the fuck were they going to do about it?

Chapter 3
Immigrants

ASSUNTA MORETTI GREW up in Sorrento, Italy, in a home overlooking the Bay of Naples. As a child, she could frequently be seen running through the acres of lemon groves her family owned with the Esposito family. Their lemons were in high demand by the area's limoncello producers. The heavy lemon fragrance that floated for miles along the Amalfi Coast was a scent that she could recall long after she came to America.

Assunta had little formal education, but as she grew into her teens she spent a great deal of time listening and learning about the family business. In 1919, at the age of sixteen, she walked down the aisle of La Chiesa de Santa Croce to marry Bruno Esposito. He was ten years older, but, as was customary at that time, it was a marriage arranged to unite the two families, combining their interests in the lemon groves. Bruno was already running most of the day-to-day operations, and both families were happy that the groves would be passed along for many generations to come.

For a while it looked like those future generations might never appear. Assunta had several miscarriages, but eventually she gave birth to a daughter, Chiara, in 1922. Chiara would be the couple's only child. More miscarriages followed, one of which was an ectopic pregnancy that caused severe blood loss and nearly killed Assunta.

The groves thrived, but early in 1925 they were infested with a fungus that left the Espositos with a paltry crop. During the spring of that year, Assunta walked in on Bruno as he sat at their simple kitchen table, his forehead resting on the heels of both hands, obviously distraught. He had made a decision that would affect the course of their lives.

Bruno lifted his head as Assunta sat across from him. "We have to leave. I am making arrangements to sail to America."

"Why do we have to leave? Is it the groves? Our families have managed to survive these things before."

"Yes, but the groves are just the final push I needed." Bruno looked into Assunta's eyes and hesitated. Assunta sat quietly, waiting for Bruno to continue. "I'm afraid for Italy's future. There has been talk that Mussolini was behind Matteotti's assassination last year, and I believe it. I don't trust that man. I think we should leave before things get worse. I spoke to Vito Andrullo—you know him, he owns Campania Limoncello. Vito is willing to buy the groves."

"Shouldn't you ask Carmine if he wants to buy us out and keep the groves in the family?"

"I did. My brother has no interest in the groves—he's happy in Naples with his barbershop, so Vito will own it all. I offered him a reasonable price. In a few years the groves will recover, and he'll be able to plant new trees. He'll do well. Vito will probably control all limoncello production in the area some day."

In retrospect, Assunta was amazed at how Bruno was able to foresee the political problems that would come over the next two decades. They left Italy before Mussolini's dictatorship and fascism consumed the country.

Taking only their necessary belongings, they boarded an ocean liner for the weeklong journey to America. When they arrived at Ellis Island, an immigration official mistakenly wrote Chiara's name as Clara on her documents, giving her a new name. Despite that glitch, which the newly dubbed Clara liked, they quickly became successful in America. Shortly after their arrival, they settled in

Newark, New Jersey, where Bruno opened a small produce market that provided the family with a modest but steady income, even during the Depression.

*   *   *   *

Sammy Giordano was christened Savino Corrado Giordano in February 1921. Born in Naples, Italy, he had a limited education; as soon as he left school, he apprenticed in a barbershop owned by Bruno's older brother, Carmine. Savino served in the army during World War II and returned to Carmine's barbershop after being discharged in 1945. He dreamed of having his own business in Naples, but he and Carmine had an agreement that Savino would not open a shop within twenty-five miles; and Carmine had ties with the local Camorra, the Neapolitan equivalent of the Mafia, to help him enforce it. Savino began thinking about moving to Taormina, on the island of Sicily, well outside the limit, to break from Carmine and get started on his own. Savino had some unfinished personal business drawing him to Taormina anyway.

Over in the United States, Clara had no prospects for marriage; she was shy, kept herself plain, and was very sheltered by Assunta. This was fine with her; she had no desire to break what was an overly strong attachment to her mother. While she was growing up, Clara's parents believed that she was mentally slow and would have difficulties making her way as an adult.

Bruno and Carmine communicated frequently through letters. Carmine told Bruno about the young barber who worked for him and wanted to make his own way in the world. In turn, Bruno mentioned his daughter's likely fate as a spinster. That led to a life-changing conversation.

Carmine grabbed Savino by the shoulder as he was preparing to leave for the day.

"I have a proposal for you." Carmine wasted no time getting to the point.

"For me? What kind of proposal?

"I know you want your own shop. And you know I won't let you open one up anywhere near here."

"Are you changing your mind?"

"Your ass I'm changing my mind. Listen, you got a girl?"

"What? No. What are you asking?"

"My brother, Bruno, in the States. He's got a daughter he wants to marry off. I haven't seen her since she was a little girl. She'd be a good catch for a guy like you. You go there and marry her, I'll see to it that you get yourself a good shop in a good location. Bruno will help with that."

"I want my own shop, yes. But get married? I don't know. I'd like to find my own wife. I don't know anything about this girl. And I want to stay in Italy. I've been thinking about Taormina."

"Let me say it another way. You can learn all you need to know about this girl. And if you don't, you're never going to have your own place in Italy. Not just near my shop, anywhere. I'll see to that."

Savino knew Carmine could make good on his threat. Frightened, he rationalized that the United States had a lot to offer. Since he had no romantic ties holding him back, Savino agreed, and Carmine and Bruno made all the plans and arrangements to unite the couple.

Savino and Clara exchanged letters and photographs for a while, creating the illusion of an actual long-distance courtship, but the resulting marriage was entirely one of mutual convenience combined with some well-placed coercion. In 1947, they were married in Newark; and Savino, his name now Americanized as Sammy, opened his barbershop on Franklin Avenue in Belleville. Sammy grew tired of Clara quickly, feeling she was neither physically nor mentally stimulating enough to sustain a long and successful life together. When his business began to thrive, he made one attempt to end the marriage, but Carmine's Camorra contacts had a long reach into Newark, and Sammy knew not to make another attempt.

Anna was born in 1950 and Tony in 1952. Clara was unable to juggle any other responsibility with raising her children; fortunately, Assunta was in the same house, ready to help her daughter handle every household chore. This constant support and lifelong sheltering made it impossible for Clara to grow into a fully functional person. She had no desire to take on any more than she felt capable of doing and was satisfied living in her self-imposed box.

Sammy and Clara settled into a boring routine and an essentially loveless marriage. Tensions flared every so often, largely out of Sammy's growing frustration with Clara's lack of physical needs. However, he never looked outside his marriage for attention, mostly out of fear that word would get to Carmine. She gave in to him as often as she felt necessary, but there was no imagination in the bedroom. Their marriage was a tinderbox, with every problem a potential fuse to ignite it.

Chapter 4
May 2003

$\mathcal{M}$Y FATHER QUIT his two- to three-pack-a-day habit over thirty years ago, but he was always complaining about being out of breath. To me, he became an older, Italian version of the boy who cried wolf. He bitched and moaned about countless aches and pains over the years. If he read an article about some disease, he had the symptoms; if one of his medications listed a potential side effect, he got it. I gradually learned to ignore what he said, sure that his doctor just humored him with various medications while secretly believing he was a hypochondriac.

Adding to his paranoia was the possibility that a new ailment would sneak up on him unexpectedly. He began to fear being more than a few miles from his house so he could be near his doctors and the local hospital, just in case he had a massive coronary, a cerebral hemorrhage, or some other catastrophe. "These things happen," he would point out. He had panic attacks if he was out of his comfort zone, sending him to the emergency room numerous times.

My mother put up with this because she had no choice, but we all felt that the old bastard had morphed from the bullying ogre he'd been into a pathetic old man. However, he still had moments of trying to bend people to his will or trying to exert some imagined authority because he had a different vision of himself. Mom still vacillated between being intimidated by him to standing up to him, but even after so many years of living with him she still never knew exactly how to act. Once I got married and had my own family, I no longer cared what he said.

My mother called me at my office about three o'clock on a Monday afternoon in early May. As controller for North Jersey Tool and Die, a small manufacturing company in Belleville, I was busy with my staff, closing the books on April's business. Because of high turnover due to experienced financial people leaving to find greener pastures, I had three entry-level accountants working for me. There were constant questions on how to handle certain transactions, and the vice president of finance was breathing down my neck, looking for detailed reports immediately. I was getting it from both ends and didn't have time for distractions.

I picked up the phone, already annoyed.

"Tony Giordano here."

"Tony, I'm at the hospital. Your father wanted me to take him to the emergency room because he was having trouble breathing."

"You're kidding—again?"

"He's being examined now."

"Well, I'm sure they'll release him, because there's nothing wrong with him—except his head. Look, Ma, I'm really busy. I'll call you tonight." I hung up and got back to work. This routine of emergency room visits would have been comical if I weren't involved.

Later that evening, I entered the house, my mind still in the office and everything that needed to be done the next day. Kathy made dinner, and we sat down to eat. Lisa was still at Princeton, preparing for her finals. The semester wouldn't be over for another two weeks. Kathy and I talked about my workday and plans we had for getting new kitchen cabinets. Washing the dishes, I told her, almost as an afterthought, about my conversation with my mother.

"You should call her. You said you would."

"They're both such pains in the ass. He's a fucking nut with all these trips to the emergency room. I can only imagine what his doctor thinks about him when these false alarms always amount to nothing. He needs a psychiatrist more than anything else. And she just humors him."

"Well, you at least should find out what's going on."

I shook my head in defeat. "I guess you're right. I'll call her as soon as we're done."

Before we finished the dishes, the phone rang. It was my mother.

"Mom, I was just about to call. Where are you?"

"We're at the hospital. Your father was admitted about six o'clock."

"That's unbelievable. They didn't send him home? What are they saying?"

"Oh, I don't know." She was upset, but I could hear in her voice that she felt this was another petty disruption in her otherwise boring life. "They want to run some more tests," she explained. "They don't like his oxygen levels or something; I don't understand what they're saying. Daddy's having trouble breathing, and he can barely speak."

I was annoyed with him, and my tone of voice reflected that. "Do you need me to come? I doubt we're going to learn anything today; it's almost eight o'clock. When are you going home?"

"Your father wants me to stay overnight."

"What a baby. Ma, you can't do that. You should sleep at home and go back tomorrow. Don't let him manipulate you into staying. Go home and go back to the hospital tomorrow. I'm sure it's nothing."

"I'll see what he wants me to do."

"No! Don't ask him what he wants—you know what he wants. Just tell him nothing's going to happen until tomorrow, and you'll go back then. Why should you be put out because of his nonsense? You know he just gets himself all worked up for some stupid little thing, and he develops these symptoms. Just go home. When he sees you're not falling for his bullshit, he'll amazingly recover."

"You're probably right."

"Look, if for some strange reason he's still in the hospital tomorrow, I'll come by after work. Then I'll talk to him and find out what his deal is. Do the doctors know about all his previous problems? Did you suggest to them it might be mental?"

"No, I didn't say anything like that," she said. "I would never bring up anything like that. That's terrible. But the tests show an oxygen problem, so maybe it's not mental."

"Ma, just go home. Call me at work if he gets released tomorrow. Otherwise I'll go to the hospital right after work."

"Okay. I will. Goodbye, Tony."

"Bye, Ma."

We hung up. I was annoyed but wasn't surprised we were going through this again. When Anna and I were growing up, he had to be the king of the castle. He demanded our respect, even though he didn't earn it. What we gave him wasn't respect but fear. Once we got older, that feeling of fear turned into ridicule, although we never explicitly showed it. By then, all he could do was try to remain the center of attention with all these phantom health issues.

Anna and I would often talk about our feelings for him. We thought he was a terrible father and had many conversations admitting we'd had the same fear of him coming into our rooms in the middle of the night and killing all of us. We hated him.

The next day, I got no call at the office from my mother. Before I left, I called the hospital. He was still there. I didn't want to ruin my evening but went to visit him as I had promised.

I walked into his room. My mother was sitting in a chair off in one corner and got up to kiss me as I walked in.

"Hi, Tony."

"Hi, Ma." I went to my father's bedside. He was either asleep or just resting with his eyes closed.

"Dad?"

He had a nasal cannula and was attached to a monitor and a saline I.V. drip. I found out he hadn't had anything to eat or drink since he'd been admitted.

He slowly opened his eyes.

"Hello, son." It always annoyed me when he called me "son" instead of Tony. I suppose I didn't want to acknowledge the reality that he was my father. His tone of voice was designed to get the maximum amount of sympathy from me.

"What are you doing in here?" I asked.

"I'm having trouble breathing." He seemed to be struggling for breath. I felt he was exaggerating for my benefit. "They say my oxygen levels are low."

"Don't struggle to talk—save your breath." I was trying to be a good son. "Just rest for now."

"They gave him a nebulizer to use twice a day," my mother added, pointing to a small device that had a long, flexible tube and a mouthpiece at the end. "It creates a mist with medicine in it that's supposed to open his air passages."

My father closed his eyes again. I turned from the bed and motioned to my mother to step out of the room. We walked into the hallway and stood just outside the doorway.

"Why do you put up with his bullshit? I can't believe the doctors didn't release him already. It's the same as always. He had a panic attack because he's afraid of everything now."

"I don't think so, Tony. They ran some more tests, and we should have the results tomorrow."

"I'll be very surprised if it's anything. I don't see any reason to stay. He's going to fall asleep, and I'm not going to stay here staring at him. You should go home, too. When did you get here?"

"First thing this morning."

"Well, go home and get a good night's rest. Enjoy it while he's not home."

"Will you come here tomorrow night?"

"I doubt he'll still be here. But what if he is—do you expect me to come every day to babysit? I've got other things to do."

"He's your father!" She spoke in a whisper, but her anger came through loud and clear.

"Yeah, right. Let's just see what the doctors say tomorrow." I peeked into the room; he appeared to be asleep. "He's sleeping," I said as I turned back toward my mother. "I'm going to go. I'll talk to you tomorrow."

By the time I got home, I was boiling, thinking about how often he used health issues to manipulate everyone. "He actually wishes these symptoms on himself," I told Kathy as we got ready for bed. "It's all in his head, and he does it just to get attention. I've got to speak to his doctor and ask him about referring him to a psychiatrist."

"What if it's really something this time? He's eighty-two, after all."

"Come on, you've been through this crap with me before. When has it ever been anything but a waste of everyone's time?"

"It's always a breathing problem. Maybe it finally developed into something serious."

"All of a sudden? He's seen doctors so many times over the years—someone would've seen something by now. I'm telling you, it's just another panic attack."

"But he's been to a psychiatrist before, and nothing came of it."

"That's because Dad stopped seeing him after two sessions. He didn't think the doctor would tell him anything he didn't already know, and he won't listen to anyone's advice, because he thinks he knows better than everyone else. If he ever really opened up to someone, he might be able to get some help."

"What makes you think he'll go to one now?"

"He probably won't go, but at least he'll know nobody believes he has a physical problem." I shook my head. "Man, I really lost the parent lottery. My father's a bastard, and my mother is clueless."

Kathy tilted her head and looked at me with a sarcastic but humorous expression. "It's amazing that with your genes, you turned out so perfect!"

We laughed. "You're right," I said. "It *is* amazing. And you are so lucky to have married me!" We turned off the lights and went to bed, holding each other.

*   *   *   *

My mother left the hospital shortly after I did and managed to get a good night's sleep. The next day, she asked me to get to the hospital as soon as I could so I could speak with the doctor before he left. We were still finishing the monthly close, but my staff had things covered pretty well, so I left a little early. When I arrived, we asked one of the nurses if Dr. Callahan could see us when he had a chance. He had already explained the test results to my mother, but she wasn't able to relay the information to me, due to both a lack of confidence in getting everything right and the fact that she certainly wouldn't have gotten everything right.

Dr. Greg Callahan looked like a doctor on a television program, distinguished, about six feet tall, with salt-and-pepper hair. My father had been seeing him for about ten years, since his previous doctor retired. At first Dad was reluctant to see him, even though the elderly Dr. Franconi had given him the highest praise, because he wasn't Italian. But surprisingly, Dad liked him immediately, and Dr. Callahan treated him with respect throughout all his panic attacks and other ailments. This was the first time I met him, and he was very straightforward. After our quick greetings, he took us to a nearby waiting room and got down to business.

"As I explained to your mother, your father underwent a series of tests under the direction of Dr. Lawrence Donnelly, a pulmonologist, one of the best in the state. He's not available at the moment, or he'd be here. He performed a lung function test, checked your father's blood oxygen levels, and took a chest x-ray. After reviewing all the test results, he determined that your father has COPD—chronic obstructive pulmonary disease."

I had never heard of that and glanced over to my mother, surprised that they'd found anything at all.

"What is that? How serious is it? Did it just develop all of a sudden? He's had tests before."

"COPD is a term that covers a few conditions. In his case it's emphysema, which you're probably more familiar with. He's had breathing difficulties for a while, as you know, but emphysema progresses gradually, so it takes a while to get to this point. He's been on various breathing medications for some time now—going back to when Dr. Franconi was treating him."

"But those things are caused by smoking, aren't they? He quit over thirty years ago."

"That may be true, but he told me that he'd smoked very heavily for over thirty years before that—starting as a teenager. That caused a lot of irreversible damage. He also told me that his barbershop was next to a dry cleaner in a strip mall. It's possible that he was breathing some fumes from the solvents that were used there. So even after he stopped smoking, his lungs were still being harmed. Dry cleaners are using different solvents now, but he was exposed for a long time."

"I always thought his breathing problems were due to his panic attacks."

"His anxiety definitely made the problem worse during an attack, but the underlying cause was the emphysema."

"What can you do for him?"

"Well, there's no cure, and, unfortunately, it's irreversible. However, we'll be more aggressive with his medication and start him on an oxygen program. He already has a nebulizer. A nurse will be in shortly to get him started on some of the meds Dr. Donnelly prescribed. That should begin to alleviate some of the discomfort. Once we see he's responding, he'll be released, and he'll just need to maintain the medication and oxygen at home."

"What can Mom and I do?"

"Just keep on top of him to follow our instructions." He smiled. "I know he can be stubborn at times."

"That's for sure. Well, thanks for everything."

"You're quite welcome."

After Dr. Callahan left, my mother and I began walking back to my father's room.

"I had no idea he was being treated for any breathing problems," I said. "He never said anything."

"He never told me, either. He always took so many pills and vitamins; I didn't know what they were for."

"You never asked anything when he came back from a doctor's visit?"

"He just said to leave him alone."

"Well, it serves him right that we never believed he had a problem. The idiot."

"Have a little respect. All we can do is pray that he gets better."

"Pray? You mean talk to yourself. You don't really believe there's an invisible man up in the sky listening, do you?"

"Yes, God is. Pray that your father gets better."

I shook my head. "Do you think God made him sick?"

"God didn't make him sick; his smoking did that. But God knew it would happen—he knows everything."

"Well, if God knew Dad was going to get sick, then why would he make him better just because we pray for it? He should have just not allowed him to get sick in the first place. Seems like a big waste of God's time to let someone get sick only to make him better again, especially with all the wars and famine and shit that should be keeping him busy."

"God wanted to teach your father a lesson. He works in mysterious ways."

"That's the standard answer when you can't justify the ridiculousness of these beliefs, isn't it? God works in mysterious ways. No, things happen because they happen, but when they're too much to handle, it's because God works in mysterious ways. Well, if he was working for me, I'd fire him."

"You're being blasphemous. I think you'd better go home and think about what you've been saying."

"Yeah, I think I've had just about enough today. We'll see what we need to do tomorrow." I walked out of the hospital and to my car, knowing that my life was about to be disrupted for quite a while.

Chapter 5
June 1960

*A*S TONY'S EIGHTH birthday approached, he was not very subtle about what gift was at the top of his list. He asked for the same thing every chance he had. The last two Christmases and birthdays offered him opportunities to make his wish known, but without success. This time he was determined to be more aggressive and successful—he wanted a dog.

Many of his friends had dogs. He loved playing with them when he was at his friends' homes. He loved the affectionate ones that would lick his face when he hugged them and rubbed their bellies. Most were mutts, but there was a dachshund, a collie, and a Chihuahua in the neighborhood, too. The Chihuahua was the only one he didn't care for. It was always barking and nipping at his heels. However, those weren't the breeds he was interested in. He wanted a cocker spaniel. He had gone to the library and took out several books about dogs, and the one about cocker spaniels really caught his attention. He liked the way they looked, and the book said they were easy to train.

Tony snuck up behind his mother while she was folding the laundry. "Mom, I know what I want for my birthday this year."

Clara looked at him, knowing what was coming. "What would you like, Tony?"

"A cocker spaniel!"

"What is that?" she teased.

"A dog! It's the best dog in the world. I read all about them."

"You know how your father feels about dogs. Didn't you ask for one before?"

"But now I know all about them. I'll take care of it, and you and Daddy won't have to do anything. I'll feed it and take it on walks and—"

"Easy, Tony. I don't want you to get your hopes up. I'm not sure about this. Let's talk to Daddy when he gets home. Maybe he'll change his mind." Clara knew there was no changing Sammy's mind, but she wanted the bad news to come from him.

Tony agreed to wait for his father and began to plot his strategy. He walked to his grandparents' side of the house and found Anna in her room, reading. The school year had just finished, and they both had a lot of time on their hands.

"Anna, I'm going to ask Daddy if I can get a dog for my birthday—a cocker spaniel."

"He hates dogs."

"Will you help me ask him? He'll listen to you."

"I've asked him before. He told me no, just like he told you before, and like he's going to tell you again."

"But maybe he'll be different this time if we ask him together."

"We're both going to get hit if we bother him about it too much. Think of something else you want for your birthday—it's not gonna be a dog."

Almost two years older, Anna was wiser, especially when it came to Sammy; but Tony wasn't about to give up. He wanted a cocker spaniel, and that was all he was focused on. He left Anna's room, went to his own room, and shut the door. He plopped down on the bed with his arms crossed behind his head and closed his eyes. He thought of the picture of the cocker spaniel he saw in the book. He imagined playing with it in the yard, rolling around on the grass, and hugging it. They would have so much fun together.

The day dragged on for Tony. He was certain his father would finally give him the answer he wanted to hear. After what seemed an eternity, Tony heard the back door open, his father making his grand entrance. He ran from his room but could only watch as Sammy entered the master bedroom and shut the door behind him. Tony waited patiently in the kitchen, watching as Clara prepared Sammy's scotch and water, a routine that went back to the beginning of their marriage.

Clara felt helpless, knowing she would be unable to prevent what was about to occur. She didn't want to tell Tony to give up his desire for a dog, and she didn't want the scene that she was sure would follow, but she did nothing. Sammy could be the villain.

Eventually Sammy emerged, passing Tony without a word and going straight for his drink, which Clara had placed in its usual spot on the kitchen table. Sammy wouldn't greet Tony first—Tony had to learn respect for his father and acknowledge his authority. Tony followed directly behind Sammy as he went to the table.

"Daddy, I think I know what I want for my birthday."

"Is that the first thing you're going to say to me?"

"No. Hi, Dad. How was work? I think I know what I want for my birthday."

Sammy turned to Clara. "Where's Anna?"

"In her room."

"Didn't she hear me come home?"

"I don't know. I guess not, or she would be here. It's hard to hear from the other side of the house. Tony, go get your sister."

Tony sensed things were not going as planned. He left and returned with Anna.

"Hi, Daddy," she said. She was already trembling inside; she knew she had made a mistake.

"I've been home for ten minutes. Where were you?"

"I was reading. I didn't hear you come in."

"Your room is on the other side of Tony's wall. I know you can hear, and besides, I'm home the same time every day." His voice was stern and getting louder. "You come and see me when I get home—don't you know that? I don't work all day so that you can ignore me."

Anna was bracing herself for a slap. It didn't come. She was holding back tears.

"I'm sorry, Daddy. It won't happen again. I hope you had a good day."

Sammy sat at the table, waiting for his dinner to be served. He wasn't an imposing figure. He stood 5'8" and weighed about 150 pounds. At thirty-nine, his full head of wavy hair was black and sleek. But even with his slight frame, he was a giant to Tony and Anna, and his tone and demeanor more than made up for his small stature. The children feared him and regretted doing anything that made him cross. Unfortunately, Tony still hadn't learned when he should hold his tongue. Unlike Anna, he always struggled with what to say and when to say it; as he got older, he tested every boundary just to get a reaction.

Clara placed a large bowl of spaghetti in the center of the table and filled everyone's dishes. They sat in silence and ate. Tony couldn't hold it in any longer.

"Daddy, I think I want a cocker spaniel for my birthday."

Sammy kept his head down, looking at his plate as he kept eating. Clara gave Tony a look that said "Not now," but it was lost on Tony. Anna tried to kick Tony's leg under the table, but she couldn't reach and decided not to slouch and make it obvious that she was trying to get his attention.

Tony continued. "I've been reading about cocker spaniels, and it would be a perfect dog for me. We'd all love him and have fun with him."

Sammy tossed his spoon and fork on the table, and they bounced onto the floor. The others cringed. Tony realized he had made a mistake, but it was too late.

Sammy glared at Tony. "Why are you such an imbecile? I told you before there will be no dogs in this house."

Tony shrank in his seat. Anna focused on her plate, not wanting to accidentally catch her father's eye, afraid she might become his next victim.

Sammy continued his tirade. "You're not going to take care of it because you're a lazy piece of shit. They're filthy and shit all over the house. Are you going to take it for walks? Are you going to take it to the vet? Are you going to pay for dog food and doctors? No. I am. They ruin a house, scratching everything and pissing on everything, and they make the house smell."

Clara felt helpless, but she knew not to challenge Sammy in front of the children, or she would be next.

"Do you want to live with filthy animals? When you get older, you can live in a barn if you want. If you ever ask me again, I'll knock your goddamn teeth out. Clara, get me another fork and spoon."

Clara got up to get the utensils, relieved that Sammy had raised only his voice, not his hands. As they quietly continued eating, Sammy looked at each of them in turn, making sure they knew the last word on the subject had been spoken. Tony was disappointed but happy that he had somehow avoided a beating; he decided the last words had yet to be said.

"How about an Erector Set?" He was grinning, but his eyes were moist.

Chapter 6
September 1963

SAMMY WAS SHIRTLESS, sitting on the living room sofa. He was nearing forty-three, and his hair was graying at the temples, but he maintained his slim physique. He had pushed the floral centerpiece on the coffee table to the side and lit six tealight candles. There were a corresponding number of small drinking glasses nearby. It was a Sunday afternoon, and eleven-year-old Tony was lying on his side on the floor between the coffee table and the television, his head supported by the palm of his hand, watching the last regular season Mets game. Sammy was a Yankees fan, so instinctively Tony liked the Mets, although their second season of existence was proving almost as futile as their first. They were in the process of being destroyed by the Houston Colt 45s, another 1962 expansion team, 13–4, to end up with a 51–111 record, which at least was an improvement from their first year. The Yankees, by contrast, were on their way to the World Series. Tony hated the Yankees mainly because his father liked them.

"Son, I need you to do something."

Tony, who had been oblivious to Sammy's activities behind him, got up and saw the candles and glasses on the table. He squinted his eyes in astonishment.

"What?"

"I'm going to lie on my stomach. Put all the candles on my back and then cover them with the glasses."

"Huh? Why?"

"Just do what I tell you."

"Where on your back?"

"Put one on each shoulder blade, and then below them about halfway down, and the last two below them just above my belt. And be careful not to drop a candle or drip any wax on the rug."

Very slowly Tony began doing as he was told, afraid he was going to set the house on fire. After he put each candle in place, he covered it with a glass. As he continued, he saw the first candles slowly extinguish; smoke filled the glasses. When he put the last glass over the candle, he stepped back.

"What do I do now?"

"Watch your game. I'll tell you when to take the glasses and candles off."

After about fifteen minutes, Sammy instructed Tony to remove the glasses. One by one he had to give a good tug to remove them, making a popping sound. He placed the glasses and candles on the coffee table. There were six circular red welts on Sammy's back. Tony couldn't believe his father would do such a thing.

"What is this for?"

"It's called Chinese cupping. It relieves back pain. It's good for the muscles and sucks out the poisons."

"Poisons?" Even at the age of eleven, Tony didn't simply accept everything he was told. "Does it hurt?"

"Not really. My back is always sore, and I read that this helps."

This was standard procedure with Sammy. He was always searching for cures that did not involve medication for every little pain he had. Medicine always had side effects, and he mistrusted doctors. He believed in shamans and their methods more. Tony decided not to pursue the conversation further, but he was feeling extremely uneasy about his father.

*   *   *   *

Clara and Anna had spent the day with Nana'Sunta and Bruno, visiting relatives. Unlike Sammy and his family, the Morettis and

Espositos were close-knit, and there were many cousins in northern New Jersey within easy driving distance. Sammy wanted no part of visiting people he didn't like, and Clara was happy not to bring her brooding husband along. Tony was spared from going so he could watch the game.

Clara, her parents, and Anna returned home about an hour after the cupping procedure was over. The Mets game and season were in the history books, and Tony had gone into his room to do homework. Sammy had fallen asleep on the couch, face down with his shirt still off. The rest of the family walked into the living room and saw Sammy lying on the couch. They quickly noticed the candles and glasses on the coffee table.

Assunta shook her head in disbelief. With a sweeping gesture, she motioned to the coffee table. "*Che assurdità è questa?*"

Clara was embarrassed. "I don't know, Ma." Bruno noticed the welts on Sammy's back and pointed at them. "This is voodoo!"

Sammy stirred and sat up. "What are you talking about?"

Anna could sense an argument about to begin. She'd seen enough of them over the years. She quietly left the room and went to find her brother.

Sammy continued, "You're all really quick to question something you don't understand. You think it's absurd? I'm open to trying new things because I have a brain and want to learn. The rest of you haven't grown mentally since you were children."

Bruno was outraged. In Italian he said, "You're a disgrace, speaking to my wife and daughter like that. And you show no respect to me, either. You do strange things in my house because you are a strange man. What is all this nonsense? Why is your back all marked? I don't know why I agreed with my brother to bring you to the United States. You've never acted like you wanted to belong to this family."

Sammy stood and responded in Italian. "You agreed because no one else was stupid enough to marry Chiara." At that, Clara burst into tears and turned to Assunta, who put her arms around her. "You're all lucky I came here." Sammy was enraged. His eyes were wide open, the veins in his neck throbbing. "I'm the one whose life is ruined. I have a wife who can't think on her own and needs to clear everything with her mother first. We're stuck in this house because Chiara can't leave her mommy. Assunta's opinion has more weight than mine by far. And you do everything Assunta wants too, Bruno. You have no backbone."

Bruno took a step in Sammy's direction, his fists clenched. Assunta took her arms from Clara and put a hand on Bruno's chest to stop him from going any farther. She looked at Sammy. "This is what you think, Savino? We bring you here to let you have a good life in America, and you turn it against us. You have a good business. You pay very little rent here, just enough to cover the taxes. Chiara gave you two beautiful children. And you have no gratitude. Go if you're not happy. Get out."

"Mama, no," cried Clara. "Sammy. Don't leave; she doesn't mean it." She placed her hands on her cheeks and shook her head, pleading with him.

"Yes, she does. See how you can cope without me, Chiara. You'll be one big happy family." He grabbed his shirt and put it on as he walked to the bedroom. Clara reached for him as he passed her, but he dodged her grasp. She followed him into the bedroom, where he opened the closet door and reached for a suitcase. He threw it on the bed and opened it, removing the smaller one nested inside and tossing it on the floor. Clara stood there crying as he began throwing clothes inside.

"Sammy, please. I love you. Think about what you're doing."

"You don't love me—you never did. You're closer to your mother than you'll ever be to me. You don't support me in anything I do. You ridicule what you don't understand."

"I didn't say anything. I don't know what you were doing in the living room, but I didn't question anything. Mama and Papa did."

"Did you tell them to stop?" He continued packing the suitcase, randomly throwing in shirts, socks, and underwear. "Did you come to my defense? No. You let them say what I was doing was absurd, and none of you even know what I was doing. You don't want to understand, and you don't care. I'll be better off by myself."

"What about Anna and Tony? What are we going to say to them?"

"I'm not saying anything. You can say whatever you want. Your mother can coach you. She's been putting words in your mouth all your life."

"You're just going to leave without seeing them?"

"They won't care. I know you and your mother have been turning them against me from the day they were born. I can tell they don't respect me. They should idolize their father."

With that, he closed the suitcase, squeezing the clothes in. He picked it up and walked out of the bedroom, passing Clara without looking at her. Assunta and Bruno were still standing in the living room. Sammy glared at them. "You were hoping this day would come, weren't you? Well, you have your daughter back, and you got rid of me. To hell with all of you!" He turned and went through the kitchen to the back door. They heard it slam behind him. Shortly after, they heard the car start, and he was gone.

*   *   *   *

Anna and Tony had been in Tony's room throughout the argument. They could hear only muffled conversation through the closed door, and since it was mostly in Italian, they didn't understand it, anyway. They did, however, sense the tone of the conversation and were afraid.

"What was Daddy doing?" Anna asked.

"Some stupid thing. He lit some candles and told me to put them on his back and put little glasses over them. They left big red marks. He's weird."

"Sounds like they're having a big fight. Daddy scares me."

"Me, too. He's always yelling and hitting us for nothing. Sometimes I think he's going to come in my room and kill me while I'm sleeping."

"I think that too, sometimes." Anna felt good that she wasn't alone in her fears. "I saw him hit Mommy once. I thought he was going to kill her, he hit her so hard."

They soon heard a door slam and thought they heard their mother crying. Tony slowly opened his bedroom door, and they both walked to the arched entryway to the living room. Assunta was holding Clara, and Bruno stood behind her, his arm around her shoulder. As the children walked up to the adults, Clara heard them, turned, squatted down, and held out her arms. Anna and Tony ran to her, and Clara wrapped her arms around them. No one knew what to say.

*   *   *   *

Sammy went to his parents' house in Paterson. He had no good alternatives. He felt no love or respect for his father and pitied his mother; however, not wanting to spend an undetermined amount of time and money at a hotel, he decided it was his best option. The next morning, his mother, Rosa, placed a cup of espresso on the kitchen table in front of him and another in front of her husband, Enzo. She then pulled a chair out for herself and sat.

"Go home now," the short, gray-haired woman advised. "The children need their father. Talk to Clara. She'll understand. Please, think about what you're doing."

"Rosa, be quiet." Enzo stared at his wife, indicating that was the last thing she was permitted to say. Enzo was rail thin, but his intense eyes struck fear into anyone who met their gaze.

"This is more than just between Savino and Clara. Assunta is the real problem." He turned his attention back to Sammy.

"You were right to challenge that old cow. That imbecile Bruno never had the *cojones*. Go back in a few days, not now. Let them stew in their own juices. When you go back, you'll be in a position of strength. Then you can lay down the law."

Sammy took his father's advice and left after dinner the third night. He didn't call first to let Clara know he was returning. Driving home, he thought of what he was going to say and the changes Clara was going to have to make if she wanted him back. He would tell Assunta to stop interfering in their lives. He was primed for a fight he was going to win. His word would be law, and he *would* be obeyed.

Sammy pulled into the driveway, which was on his side of the duplex, the brakes screeching as he stopped the car. He got out, opened the trunk, grabbed his suitcase, and then slammed the trunk shut. The screen door to the porch was unlocked. When he got to the back door of the house, Sammy could see through the window that the lights were out. He turned the handle, but the door was locked. He reached for his keys, felt for the right one, put it in the keyhole and turned. Nothing. Sammy turned on the porch light and checked to make sure he had the key for the back door, which he did. He tried again, unsuccessfully. His anger rising, he banged on the door with his fist.

"Clara," he screamed. "Open the goddamn door! Clara!" He continued banging on the door and screaming until finally he saw the kitchen light come on. Clara opened the door. As soon as it was slightly ajar, Sammy kicked it with the bottom of his left foot, slamming it into the wall.

"You couldn't wait to change the locks, could you?"

"I'm sorry, Sammy," Clara pleaded. "Mama thought it was a good idea."

"Mama thought," Sammy repeated. "Do you ever have a thought of your own? It didn't work too good, though, did it? I'm in."

Sammy stormed in and furiously paced back and forth in the small confines of the kitchen, his eyes on Clara.

"Sammy, don't be mad. Let's work this out." She tried to grab his arm so he would stop pacing and sit down, but he pulled away.

"Oh, we'll work this out, all right. There are going to be some changes around here."

"No, Sammy, let's just go back to the way things were. You're back now. Everything can go back to normal."

"There's going to be a new 'normal' around here," Sammy said, and he laid out the conditions for his return. "We're leaving this house as soon as possible. I'll start looking for our own place tomorrow."

"Where, Sammy? Everything is here. The kids' school, your shop."

"Somewhere in town, but as far away from your parents as we can get. I'd move to another state if I could. I don't want you or the kids seeing your parents any more than is absolutely necessary."

"But, Sammy, they love the children and are very good to them. And you know how much my mother helps me with them."

"Do you want me back? I'll turn right around and leave again. You need me more than I need you, and you know it. This is how it's going to be."

"Why? What have they done?" Clara was crying, but Sammy felt no sympathy for his wife. He knew he was in complete control.

"They're a bad influence, turning the kids against me. You have to make sure Anna and Tony understand what a good father I am and that they have to respect me."

Clara didn't know what to do or say. She needed her parents, especially Assunta, but didn't want a broken marriage, so she gave in. She hoped that in time she'd find a way around these new demands.

Within three months, Sammy found and purchased a split-level home. Clara went with him to each house being considered, but in reality she had no input.

"What do you think of this one?" Sammy asked as they looked at the kitchen. The realtor stepped outside to give them some privacy.

"Well, the bedrooms upstairs are a little small, and the kitchen needs some work."

"It's in as good a location as I'm going to find. I'm making an offer."

The house was on the other side of town, reasonably close to his shop but still too close to his in-laws, in Sammy's opinion. There wasn't much he could do about that, short of relocating his business or having a longer commute. He knew Clara would visit Assunta with the kids as often as she could get away with it. He'd just have to keep on top of her, calling her throughout the day to make sure she was home; if she wasn't, she'd have to be able to account for her whereabouts. He was winning this war, or else.

Chapter 7
June 2003

AFTER NEARLY A month in the hospital, my father wasn't showing any progress or any desire to help himself. Dad was now using the nebulizer four times a day and was constantly attached to the nasal cannula that he'd been given when he was first admitted. However, his stubborn streak undermined any good the additional oxygen provided, since he refused to get out of bed to walk along the hospital corridors, even though the nurses insisted the exercise would be good for him.

Watching him inhale his medication along with the steam produced by the nebulizer didn't make me feel any sympathy for him. The excess vapors surrounded his head as he sucked on the hookah-like device, and I could think only of how ridiculous he looked. I felt he was getting his payback. *How the mighty have fallen,* I thought. He was the only one to blame for his situation getting to this stage.

My mother continued to spend most of every day with him, sitting in his room in almost complete silence. I couldn't understand that level of devotion, especially after all he had put her through over the years. It was obvious to me she had nothing better to do.

Visiting him every day after work and on weekends would have been a waste of my time. When it became clear that because of his lack of progress he wouldn't be released any time soon, I decided to limit my visits as much as possible. One or two times a week were all I could take of staring at him. Any more time with him would just increase my aggravation.

One Saturday in mid-June, when Lisa's semester was over, she was back home and joined us for a visit. She was smart enough to know that she should see her grandfather in the hospital once in a while, even though he'd never been the grandfatherly type. As we drove there, she was honest about her feelings.

"You know I'm only going so he'll have one less thing to complain about, don't you?"

"We won't stay long," Kathy replied. "Although even if we stayed five hours, it probably wouldn't be long enough for him." Kathy was the family diplomat and always said the right things around my parents, but she was well aware of their shortcomings. She always tried to give them the benefit of the doubt, even though they usually let her down.

"Believe me, sweetheart, I won't drag you there any more than is absolutely necessary," I added.

*   *   *   *

Arriving at my parents' house on Christmas Day in 1979, Kathy and I sat in the car for a few minutes before getting out. The early afternoon air was crisp, and the clear blue sky added to the sense that we'd have an unusually pleasant holiday with my family. I had reason to hope it would be better than the disastrous holiday dinners that had taken place as far back as my memory could reach. We had just found out the week before that Kathy was pregnant, and we had decided to break the news at dinner.

"I'm nervous," she told me. "I'm afraid of how they're going to react."

"They'll be fine. You're carrying their first grandchild. Who wouldn't be thrilled?" I reassured her as well as I could, although I wasn't sure what to expect, either. We were entering uncharted territory.

I helped Kathy out of the car and put my arm around her as we walked toward the front door. "I think we're going to be surprised by their reaction."

My mother greeted us with hugs and kisses, and my father awkwardly shook my hand and kissed Kathy on the cheek. He didn't seem to notice as she instinctively tensed up.

"Something to drink?" he asked.

"I'll just grab a beer from the fridge," I said.

"Wine for you, Kathy? We have that Chablis you like."

Alcohol hadn't entered our thoughts. We had planned on telling them at dinner, but Kathy refusing a glass of Chablis at Christmas would have to be explained. I looked at Kathy, tilted my head, and lifted my eyebrows, indicating that this was probably the time. She nodded.

"Well, Dad, Mom. We were going to tell you later, but now might be better. Kathy shouldn't have any wine for a while. She's pregnant."

My mother was ecstatic. She embraced Kathy and then me, tears running down her cheeks. "Finally," she said, "we're adding to the family instead of subtracting." Anna's death still weighed on her heavily.

My father greeted the news with his usual air of skepticism. He looked at us, shaking his head. "You're still kids yourselves. What do you know about being parents?"

"Dad, we're twenty-seven. We're hardly kids." We still were standing. Kathy was trying to hold back her anger. She took my hand and squeezed it with all her strength, releasing her frustration.

"What did you two know when you had Anna?" I had no problem letting him know how I felt. "Did you read a manual first? Somehow, I think we'll do all right. Besides, I don't think you've exactly perfected the art of being a parent. I'm sure I learned something from your mistakes."

"We did our best with you and Anna," my mother said defensively. "You turned out all right."

Although my comment had been mostly directed at my father, I thought it best to change the direction of the conversation. "We'll do just fine. Look, let's try to enjoy the day and not dwell on this." I knew it was an impossible request, and the day ended up the same as every other Christmas.

* * * *

My father's attitude about the pregnancy didn't change. Luckily there were no complications, and Lisa was a beautiful, healthy baby. My father's forced smiles were obvious the one time he visited Kathy in the hospital, and he didn't want to hold Lisa, giving the lame excuse that he was afraid to drop her.

There were mixed blessings as Lisa grew up. My mother and Nana'Sunta were very helpful during Lisa's early years. One or both of them would babysit when Kathy and I had a much-needed night out, and Lisa stayed with my parents when we were able to take a short vacation. Lisa always complained about staying with them. When she was alone with my mother during the day, she wasn't allowed to go outside and play with the other kids on the block. My mother overprotected Lisa the way Nana'Sunta had overprotected her. After hearing these stories when we returned from our vacations, I would tell my mother there was no need to treat Lisa like a precious Hummel figurine and keep her cooped up in the house, but the next time we went away, it was the same old story.

My father was aloof with Lisa whenever she was in his presence, whether it was during a normal visit or a weeklong babysitting stay. He never got physical with her or gave her any verbal abuse, like he did with Anna and me, but he treated Lisa with the attitude that she owed him respect simply because he was her grandfather. He was never affectionate or playful with her while she was growing up, although he expected her to voluntarily approach him with hugs and kisses. None of this came as a surprise to me, but it hurt both Lisa and Kathy.

In addition, my parents were as frugal with Lisa as they were with themselves and had been with me and Anna; they did nothing with her that most grandparents did with their grandchildren. There was nothing Lisa considered fun about the prospect of spending any time with them. It was no wonder that as a young woman, those memories lingered in her mind, giving her little sympathy for my father and no desire to visit him in the hospital.

*   *   *   *

When Kathy, Lisa, and I got to Dad's room, my mother was in her usual perch in the corner. Even though their insurance would cover only a semiprivate room, my father preferred to be alone, because a stranger in the same room would annoy him. So my mother requested a private room when he was admitted, even though they had to pay the difference out of pocket.

"Ma, why do you have to spring for a private room for him? Let him share a room. You're only feeding into his idea that he's special." I tried to reason with her unsuccessfully.

She'd made the right decision, though. It was a small price to pay to avoid more complaints. No one expected he'd be in the hospital this long, however, and the tab was adding up.

My father was in bed with his head elevated, watching one of the twenty-four-hour news channels. We went to his bedside, maneuvering around the adjustable bed table and equipment cords. In turn, Lisa and Kathy leaned in to greet him with a kiss. I simply patted him on the shoulder.

"How are you feeling today?" I asked.

"The same." His voice was still weak.

"The nurses are still telling him he should walk, but he doesn't want to try," my mother informed us.

"I'm too weak."

"You've got to try, Sammy. Do the best you can."

"What the hell does that mean?"

"It means you're not getting out of here unless they see some progress," I chimed in. "You want to go home, don't you?"

My mother shifted in her seat.

"Dad, why don't you just make an attempt?" Kathy said. "At least you'll know exactly what you can do, and the doctors will have some kind of benchmark to check your progress."

"Nobody knows how I feel except me. I have no strength." His voice was weak, but his anger came through loud and clear. He glared at all of us as he looked around the room, and that meant the conversation was over. With that, he closed his eyes.

I motioned with my head to everyone to leave the room. Once

we were out of my father's earshot, I looked at my mother and could see she was agitated.

"You okay?" I asked.

"I don't want him home until he's better. I can't take care of him."

"He can't stay indefinitely, Ma," Kathy said. "He's got to show some progress."

"He'll have to show a lot of progress. The nurses need to bathe him, and he's barely eating. If I have to be his nurse, I'll get sick. I'm too old for this."

"What are the options if he doesn't show some improvement?" I asked.

"Some of the nurses have told me that since he hasn't made any progress so far and isn't willing to help himself, staying at St. Luke's much longer won't make a difference. And since I can't care for him at home, he'd probably be better off in a nursing home. We'd have to pay for it, though, because he'll probably use up all the days our insurance allows."

"That's nice of him. He's going to make you destitute."

"We'll be able to afford it for a while," she assured me. Their years of frugality had finally come in handy. "They also gave me a list of places in the area that might be good," she continued. "Could you come with me tomorrow to look at them?"

I agreed to help find a place that would be convenient for her to visit and would provide good care for my father—without sending her to the poorhouse.

Since my father had decided to become uncommunicative, it was a good opportunity to leave, much to Lisa's relief. The next day, my mother and I went to three local facilities. Even though it was Sunday, they all had someone available to give a tour and answer questions. Of the three, Tranquil Meadows Adult Residence in nearby Bloomfield seemed to be the most ideal, if we were forced to go with that option. It had a nice setting, as its name would suggest; a top-notch staff; and plenty of amenities for someone who wanted to make use of them. More importantly, there were several beds available, assuming a transfer was made fairly quickly.

"I'd say this one was the best," I said to my mother as I started the car. "We're probably going to have to move him soon." There was still an outside chance that he would start cooperating with the nurses and do what was needed to regain his strength, but I wasn't betting on it.

"It just seems like everyone is giving up on him." My mother sounded melancholy, as if she were feeling sorry for him.

"He gave up on himself. It's as if he has a death wish. Or maybe it's just some perverted way to make himself the center of attention."

"He's not going to be happy about this."

"Well, that's just too bad. Maybe it's the kick in the ass he needs."

On Monday, I decided to go to St. Luke's directly after work, just to see if there was any change; I was still hoping my mother could avoid the expense of an open-ended stay in a nursing home. Of course, Dad had something to say about our quick departure on Saturday and my failure to visit on Sunday. We were alone in the room; my mother had gone to the nurses' station to tell them about our trip to Tranquil Meadows.

"I expected more from you and your family." His face had been flushed in anger since the moment I walked into the room.

"What are you talking about?" I said as I sat down. My tone was meant to indicate that I wasn't going to take any crap.

"You didn't spend two minutes here the other day and didn't come at all yesterday. What kind of son are you?"

"The kind that's got better things to do than watch you sleep because you're pissed at the world. You closed your eyes and basically said you were done talking, so we left. And didn't Mom tell you we looked at some assisted-living places yesterday? That's where you'll be going if you don't change your attitude. The hospital won't keep you forever, and you're not going home in this condition."

"I'm not going anywhere. The cocksuckers here don't listen to me. No one listens to me."

"Just the opposite—you're the one who doesn't listen to anyone. You've been hearing from day one that you've got to eat better and get a little more active."

"You eat this shit. And I don't have the strength to walk—even a little."

"Then you'll be going into a nursing home very soon instead of your own home. It's only going to be another week or so. And unless you start cooperating in a nursing home to do what you need to do to get your strength back, you're never going home. Mom can't take care of you, and Kathy and I won't. There's no excuse for you to be like this."

"I'm going home. Tell them to let me out of here."

"I'm not telling anybody anything. You tell them by acting like you should in order to get released. Otherwise, you'll have to get used to being in a home." I was enjoying giving him a hard time. Some people might call it tough love. It was tough, all right, but without the love.

My mother walked in, looking concerned.

"Sammy, Renee the nurse told me it may be necessary to transfer you someplace else by the end of next week."

"Which one's Renee?"

"The pretty black girl."

"That *mulignan* is the most useless one of the bunch. She doesn't know what she's talking about."

"Sammy, stop talking like that! She's very good, and she's trying to help so you can stay here and maybe go home. She said if you do what you're supposed to and they see that you're improving, you could stay. If not, they feel you'll be better off in another facility."

My mother was wasting her breath. He had no intention of doing anything to help his situation. The following Wednesday, with no change in his health or his attitude, we went back to Tranquil Meadows to work out the details of his transfer.

Friday was moving day. I didn't bother taking any time off from work to be there. I had no desire to witness the scene he was sure to create. After work, I went to Tranquil Meadows to see how he was handling his new home. In order to keep expenses down, he no longer had a private room and was now sharing one with a man named Leonard Klein.

Although the room had the typical hospital equipment, it was decorated more like a bedroom in one's home, presumably so it would be less frightening for the residents (they didn't use the word "patient," even in the medical section). Art reproductions were on the walls in the rooms as well as the corridors. Each resident had a small dresser and nightstand, and there was a large closet in the center of the room that was divided in two. My father insisted that the curtain separating the two beds always be drawn closed. He wanted no interaction with his roommate.

Mr. Klein's bed was closest to the door; I found out later that he'd had the opportunity to move by the window when that bed became available, but he had decided to stay where he was. When I entered the room for the first time, he nodded at me, and we exchanged a simple greeting as I crossed the room. My mother was sitting in a green sleeper at the far side of Dad's bed, next to the window. She started to rise, but I motioned to her to stay in her seat. As usual, the television was on a news channel, and they were both silently staring at the screen.

I stood at the other side of the bed, the curtain at my back. "How do you like your new home?" I asked, with just the slightest trace of sarcasm. I was looking forward to hearing how miserable he was.

My father gestured with his head, motioning to his roommate on the other side of the curtain. "Be better without the Jew," he said under his already weak breath. My mother looked horrified, afraid Mr. Klein might have heard; but both televisions were on, and the combination of the different programs and my father's weak voice made that fairly unlikely.

"Well, if you're smart, you'll start doing the rehab program like you should have been doing all along and get yourself to a point where you can go home. Until then, deal with it." I turned to my mother. "Has a doctor seen him to give him his options?"

"A doctor came in, I forget his name, some odd Indian name, and went over his records. He said he should have been able to go home from the hospital, but his lungs are worse now because he's just been lying in bed. He said he hears some rattling, and there's danger of pneumonia." I looked at my father and shook my head. My mother continued, "And some social director or something came in to tell him about the programs they had here, bingo and other games and things like that. They have a nice dining room if he wants to use it."

"Well, Dad, the ball's in your court. Maybe it's time to use some common sense and get yourself out of here." He continued to stare at the television with a look of disgust and frustration on his face. I moved to the other side of the bed and sat on the arm of the chair my mother was in. We talked about Kathy and Lisa and some other topics for about a half hour, while my father just continued to stare silently at the television. By then I'd had enough and got up.

"I'm gonna go." I gave my mother a kiss and turned to my father. "Give it some thought. You're only hurting yourself." I walked across the room and turned to Mr. Klein as I passed his bed. "Good night, Mr. Klein."

"Good night, young fella." He had a friendly smile and waved his hand.

He seemed like a nice guy.

Chapter 8
February 1972

*A*S FAR BACK as anyone could remember, students had dubbed Reynolds University in Newark the "concrete campus." It was one of three campuses Reynolds had in New Jersey. Built in the inner city in the early 1960s, a few years before the riots engulfed Newark, it included seven concrete buildings housing classrooms and labs, all surrounding a concrete plaza, with several dozen trees scattered throughout. In addition to Reynolds, Tony had been accepted to Boston University and Dartmouth, schools he would have preferred to attend for their academic reputations and their ability to get him out of the house. However, Sammy insisted he go to Reynolds because it was a state university and he would save on tuition and housing. Sammy could also make sure Tony was home each night so he could keep an eye on him. Tony was grateful that Reynolds had an excellent business and accounting curriculum, which was his planned area of concentration. It eased the blow of not attending the other schools, and, besides, Sammy thought accounting would be a good career path.

During Tony's first semester in the fall of 1970, he pledged Phi Upsilon Kappa fraternity and quickly became immersed in every aspect of Greek life. He took full advantage of the older brothers' advice on teachers and classes to take or avoid, as well as the archive of term papers that were recycled year after year. Each paper was carefully catalogued, so the brothers knew which teacher had already seen it, and when. Occasionally, a brother wrote a new paper because an adequate one did not already exist, and the collection grew.

At first Tony was shocked by what he felt was a liberal use of alcohol and drugs by the brothers and other people he knew at Reynolds. When he was in high school, he'd heard rumors that some of his friends were smoking marijuana or doing other things, but he never saw anything firsthand. Partly because he had a reputation as a "good kid" and partly because of his own naiveté, he was never offered anything and was otherwise oblivious to what was going on around him. Once he got to Reynolds, however, blatant drug and alcohol use was a badge to be worn proudly.

While he was still a pledge, he and the other would-be brothers were sent on a scavenger hunt. They were ordered to go to Poland, New York, and return with items that would prove they had been there: street signs, stationery from the local police and fire departments, a diner menu, and anything else they could find. The drive was long and boring, and there was an air of tension among the pledges; they believed they might be blackballed if they came back empty-handed. To ease their anxiety, Kenny, whose shoulder-length hair and laid-back attitude made him seem the most experienced when it came to drugs, surprised no one when he reached into his jacket pocket and pulled out a fat joint.

"Fuck it," he said, lighting it. "This is bullshit, but I might as well enjoy myself." Exhaling, he held the joint out to Tony, who was squeezed in the middle of the backseat next to him. Tony looked at it and then at Kenny.

"No, thanks. Give it to Hank," he said, gesturing with his thumb to the pledge on his right.

"C'mon. What are you, a pussy?"

"No, it's just …"

"Give it a try. I guarantee you'll like it," Kenny said, and the other pledges joined in the taunting. Tony hesitated, but Kenny rushed him. "Take it all-fuckin'-ready. You're wasting some good shit."

Giving in to the pressure, Tony gingerly took the joint from Kenny, put it to his lips, and inhaled deeply, immediately coughing and sputtering.

"Hey, don't spit on it, for fuck's sake," Hank said as he reached for it. The joint made its way around the car and back to Tony, who had recovered. Feeling a little bolder this time, he took another hit and passed it along. Soon he started feeling a bit lightheaded, but it was a pleasant feeling. The scavenger hunt was a bust, but Tony became closer to the other pledges on the trip and found a new hobby in the process.

Eventually, Tony tried everything that was offered to him: hash, Quaaludes, LSD, and other substances that were all readily available. Various combinations of drugs and alcohol left Tony violently ill more than once during his first year at Reynolds. After his baptism by fire, however, he became relatively conservative in his drug use. After one too many nights of vomiting, he restricted himself to beer or marijuana and stayed away from anything he perceived as too risky. He also made sure he got high only in the evenings and on weekends, unlike some brothers, who attended classes in a mental fog.

*   *   *   *

The acronym for Phi Upsilon Kappa was proudly pronounced "fuck" by the brothers. Over the years, the legend grew as to how the founding brothers had managed to get their name approved by the Intrafraternity Council when they applied for their charter. Occasionally the letters a fraternity uses are an acronym for some sage advice, so the application stated that they stood for "*facto ultimato karpe*," liberally translated as "seize the ultimate facts" or, more to the point, "seek the truth." The council bought it. In reality, it just meant "fuck."

Lincoln Street, which extended from the southern end of the campus, included ten former storefronts with second-floor apartments, each floor now housing either a fraternity or sorority. Phi Upsilon Kappa was in the storefront floor of one of these buildings, with a sorority, unimaginatively called Beta Beta Beta, upstairs. Being in this former storefront meant that there were no real living facilities other than a toilet and sink. There were no showers or bedrooms for any brother who needed to spend a night there to sleep off excessive partying. An old mattress had been thrown in what once had been a storeroom. If someone needed a shower, one of the sorority sisters might allow him to use their facilities. If not, a quick splash of English Leather under each arm would have to do.

One cold Friday night in February, Tony and a dozen other brothers were in the frat house. This was the usual group of brothers who would spend their weekend evenings there. Three games of poker were being played at tables spread out on the open floor. The brothers were sitting on wooden folding chairs; an old, stained couch rested against one wall, and some rickety end tables were on either side of it. Completing the minimalist décor, an old pinball machine dubbed "Typhoid Mary" stood in a corner near the entrance.

The brothers at the card tables were at the bottom of the fraternity's unique identification system. The members of Phi Upsilon Kappa were placed in subgroups that defined their sexual prowess by three different modes of transportation. A Rocket was a brother who was very smooth with women; dated as many different ones as possible, all of them very attractive; had no problem having sex with any of them; and discarded them just as easily. A Steamboat had a steady relationship with one girl and stayed monogamous. Then there were the Garbage Trucks, the group that Tony and his poker-playing buddies were in. These brothers dated occasionally; rarely had more than one or two dates with the same woman; and mostly spent their time at the frat house, getting high and playing cards.

Tony dealt a hand of seven-card stud, follow the whore, as all the queens were called, thinking he should be on a date instead of playing cards with the other Garbage Trucks, but he always seemed to get tongue-tied when he met someone. He was particularly upset that at nineteen, his penis had been used only for peeing and masturbating and had never been anywhere near a vagina.

"You dealt Lou a whore, my six is wild," yelled Barry. "You're supposed to call that. What are you, high?"

"Yeah, actually, I am." Tony laughed and took a long swig from a bottle of Rolling Rock, followed by a toke on a joint that had found its way back to him after circling the table. Everyone found this to be hysterical and couldn't stop laughing. The brothers at the other tables laughed too, having no idea why.

The games continued for a few hours, misdeals following spilled beers accompanied by inane laughter. The needle of an old record player was stuck on one groove of "In Memory of Elizabeth Reed" by the Allman Brothers, but no one noticed or could be bothered to move it. Around eleven o'clock, the front door opened, letting in a gust of cold air along with two Rockets, Randy and Brian. Between them was a black woman, probably in her late thirties or early forties; they had their arms around her.

"Hey, boys," announced Randy. "This is Bernice. Brian and I stopped at McGinley's for some brewskis. We met Bernice there and negotiated a good group rate with her. Five bucks for a BJ or ten bucks a fuck. I'm sure you Trucks will be very happy to make her acquaintance."

Randy was obviously being condescending, but the Garbage Trucks were too horny to care or even notice. They couldn't believe their luck. Randy led Bernice to the storeroom where the mattress was kept. "Me and Brian are one and two. The rest of you can line up against the wall if you're interested."

Chairs fell as the brothers leaped up to get in line; the vibrations from their movements caused the needle on the record to jump and continue playing the album. They all jostled for position, but Tony, not being very aggressive, ended up next to last, in front of Lou, the only pledge there that night. It took no more than ten minutes for each brother to go in and come back out. Every so often Bernice would come out and walk to the bathroom, naked. Her mouth was closed tight, and her cheeks were puffed out. She didn't bother to close the door, and the brothers watched as she spit into the sink. She then ran the water, filling her hand and bringing the water to her mouth, swishing it around and spitting it out. Then she walked back to the storeroom, taking the next brother in with her.

Tony turned to Lou. "You got an extra rubber?"

"No, man, I just got the one I've been carrying in my wallet for I don't know how long."

He called to the brothers in the room. "Anybody got a rubber I can use?"

"No, but we got some plastic sandwich bags and rubber bands," said Brian. That got a good laugh out of everyone.

"Just get a blowjob," advised Lou. "That'll be safe."

Finally, the storeroom door opened. Barry came out in his underwear, carrying his clothes. It was now Tony's turn. He walked in, closed the door, and saw Bernice lying on the mattress. He stood there, staring at her.

Bernice asked, "What's it gonna be? You want to get laid or you want me to suck on your little pecker?"

Tony remembered Lou's advice, but he didn't know when he'd have another chance. His head was in a heavy fog. "G-get laid. I don't have a rubber, though."

Bernice looked at him and smiled. "You a virgin, ain't you?"

"Yeah."

"My, my. That's okay. I know you clean. I clean too, honey. And I know I ain't gonna get pregnant. Gimme the ten dollars now, boy, so we got no hassles later."

Tony reached for his wallet, handed her the money, and then just stood there.

"Whatcha waitin' for, boy? Take them clothes off."

Tony fumbled with his shirt buttons.

"Don't be takin' all night, now."

Tony sped up, but he didn't get any more dexterous. Piece by piece he tossed his clothing to the floor, finally removing his underwear. He knelt on the mattress and positioned himself between Bernice's legs. Tony inched closer on his knees but didn't know what to do. Bernice sensed this and took him in her hands. In no time, Tony was ready. Bernice slid toward him and guided him in. Tony penetrated and instinctively moved his hips back and forth. He ran his eyes over Bernice's body. He noticed she was missing some teeth, and the ones she had were badly discolored. Her breasts were emaciated, with small misshapen nipples that seemed to have been chewed.

Her eyes were yellow where they should have been white. Needle marks covered her arms. Tony saw all this, but none of it registered; his brain was swimming. In about two minutes, Tony felt a surge, shuddered, and was done. He pulled out, and Bernice reached for some tissues, handed a few to Tony, and kept some for herself. As they were cleaning, she asked, "Anybody else out there?"

"Uhh, one more."

"Well, grab your clothes and get him in here. You can get dressed outside."

Tony quickly gathered his clothes, stumbled out of the storeroom, and told Lou to go in. He finished getting dressed and sat at one of the tables, dazed. Somehow, he wasn't as satisfied as he thought he would be.

*　　*　　*　　*

Early Sunday morning, Tony woke up and went to the bathroom. As he peed, it felt as if shards of glass were shooting from his penis. The pain was unbearable. He stopped the stream and went back to bed in a cold sweat. Panic set in as he linked this experience to Bernice and the night at the frat house. *What if I caught something from her?* he thought. Now, with a clearer head, he remembered her yellow eyes and the needle marks. She'd said she was clean, but come on; she was a ten-dollar whore from Newark. *Tony, you moron, what the fuck were you thinking?* he said to himself. *I finally get laid, and now I'm going to die.*

He needed to finish urinating, but he was afraid of the pain. *Maybe it'll go away by itself.* Tony went back to the bathroom. He couldn't hold it in. He gritted his teeth, wincing as he finished emptying his bladder. The stream looked milky and thicker than normal. The pain was intense. He returned to bed, wondering what he was going to do. He couldn't ignore it, but there was no way he could talk to his mother about what was happening and, more importantly, why it was happening. He thought of calling some of his fraternity brothers, but knew he was the only one who hadn't worn a condom. They'd be useless in a medical situation, anyway. He had no choice but to go to Sammy.

Tony stayed in bed for what seemed like hours. He felt weak, which scared him even more. When he heard some activity downstairs, he emerged into the hallway. Anna's door was closed; she was probably still sleeping. He went downstairs to see where his parents were and what they were doing. Sammy was sitting at the kitchen table alone, sipping his morning cup of espresso. Clara was in their bedroom, stripping the bed. Not knowing what to expect, he walked into the kitchen and stood next to his father. He took a deep breath.

"Dad?"

Sammy placed his cup on the table and looked up at Tony. "You look like shit. What's wrong?"

"Can we go in your den? I need to talk to you."

Sammy gulped down the rest of his of espresso and rose. Tony sheepishly followed him to his den. Tony sat in an old recliner that had been placed awkwardly in the corner of the room when a newer one had taken its place in the living room. His father sat behind a wooden desk that a customer had sold him secondhand. There were piles of folders on the desk and floor containing old bills, bank statements, and other papers. A small metal filing cabinet in one corner was stuffed. Sammy never threw anything away, and the room reflected Sammy and Clara's frugal ways. It had become the dumping ground for any stray piece of furniture that didn't belong anywhere else. Sammy's den could have been much nicer than the one he'd had at his in-laws' house if it hadn't been so cluttered.

"What's your problem, now?" Sammy leaned in, his arms folded on top of the desk.

"I think I'm sick. This morning, I went to the bathroom, and it hurt real bad when I peed."

"What did it feel like?"

"I don't know. It burned. It felt like a blowtorch."

That description had a familiar ring to it from Sammy's army days. He had never experienced it, but some of his buddies had.

"What have you been doing at night when you hang out with your imbecile college friends? You get high and do stupid things, don't you?"

Tony knew this wasn't going to be easy. Why would he expect any sympathy from his father now, when he'd never gotten any before? His only option was to put all his cards on the table. Leaving out the marijuana use, he described everything—being drunk, Bernice, not using a condom, everything.

Sammy stared at Tony as he spoke. His first comment was, "You fuck a ten-dollar whore and go in bareback? Now I know you're stupid."

"Dad, I know. I'm sorry. But this is where I am now. What am I gonna do?"

"Go to a doctor and get tested. If you don't, and you have the clap, you'll die, as simple as that." What Sammy lacked in bedside manner he made up for with matter-of-factness. Tony sat silently, not knowing how to respond. His father was right this time—he *was* stupid.

"Listen, it's Sunday morning. Dr. Franconi won't be available, but I'll call and get his answering service and see what they can do." Sammy rummaged around in one of his desk drawers, pulled out a beat-up address book, and leafed through it. He found the number, picked up the phone on his desk, and dialed. All Tony could think of as Sammy was dialing was that he couldn't believe his father didn't have Dr. Franconi's number memorized, considering all the times he'd called him for his own problems.

When someone picked up, Sammy gave a quick explanation of why he needed the doctor to get back to him as soon as possible. When he hung up, he looked at Tony. "Now we wait for Franconi to call back. In the meantime, take a shower, get dressed, and do what you would normally do. Don't drink anything so you won't have to pee so much. I won't say anything to your mother; she'll only get overexcited anyway."

"Thanks, Dad." Tony headed back to his room, passing his mother along the way. She was carrying a basket full of clothes and bed linens to the laundry room.

"What are you doing downstairs? You're not even dressed."

"Nothing, Mom. I just had to ask Dad something." Tony kept walking to his room.

Early in the afternoon, Sammy was in his den, listening to his favorite opera. The aria "La Donna e Mobile" from *Rigoletto* filled the room. His eyes were closed and he was holding his cittern, lightly strumming it with his thumb, as the music swept over him. The phone rang, jolting him from his reverie. He grabbed the receiver in the middle of the first ring to make sure Clara didn't pick it up, in case it was Dr. Franconi. It was. Sammy gave the doctor the details of Tony's problem and managed to get an appointment at nine o'clock Monday morning. Luckily, the barbershop was closed Mondays, and Sammy knew it wouldn't be the first time Tony would skip a class or two.

*　　*　　*　　*

Monday morning, Sammy took Tony aside so Clara couldn't hear their conversation.

"You know where Dr. Franconi's office is, don't you?"

"Yeah. I've been there before."

Like a master spy, Sammy laid out his plan. Part of him wanted to improve what he knew was a horrible relationship with his son; he hoped Tony would finally realize what a good father he was. Also, keeping a secret from Clara was something he enjoyed. Knowing things she didn't made him feel superior.

"Since you should be in school, we'll take separate cars so your mother doesn't get suspicious. I'll leave a few minutes after you. Wait for me outside the building, and we'll go in together." The only thing he left out was synchronizing their watches.

"Okay." Tony couldn't believe the trouble Sammy was going through to keep his situation from his mother. He was beginning to feel grateful that his father would do this for him. Maybe he had a soft side after all.

Dr. Franconi's office was ten minutes away. Tony and Sammy met shortly before nine. They checked in with the receptionist and waited. It was nine forty-five before Tony was called in; the waiting added to his anxiety. Tony and Sammy followed the pretty blonde nurse into an examination room, where she took his temperature and blood pressure. Tony couldn't help but look at her as she did her work. She made him more uncomfortable, considering why he was there. He was glad she didn't need to know. She had his records, which consisted of only a few pages; he didn't see the doctor very often.

"What brings you in to the doctor's office this morning?"

Tony's face turned beet red. "We told him yesterday," he shot back.

"Well, can you tell me?" she asked sweetly. "I'd like to get your records updated before Dr. Franconi comes in. That way he'll be totally prepared."

"I ... well ..."

"It burns when he's urinating. He may have the clap." Sammy didn't mince words.

"I see," she said, looking at Tony. Her eyes were wide with shock at Sammy's bluntness. She hastily scribbled a few things in the file. "I know Dr. Franconi will need a urine sample." She retrieved a cup from a cabinet. "Fill about a third of this. The bathroom is just down the hall on your right. Leave the cup on top of the tank, and let me know when you're done. I'll be at the front desk. Then come back here. Dr. Franconi will be in shortly." She patted Tony on his knee as she rose. "Don't worry. Dr. Franconi will take good care of you."

Tony filled the cup as he was told, wincing through the pain, and returned to the room. Another twenty minutes passed before Dr. Franconi opened the door. In his sixties, with a full head of wavy gray hair, the doctor looked like a wise old man. The few times Tony had seen him, he'd liked him, so he started feeling a little less uneasy.

"Your father told me you had an encounter that may have left you with an unintended souvenir, is that right?"

"I guess. It burns like crazy when I urinate."

"Any discharge?"

"I'm not sure. It looks a little thick and cloudy."

"Your urine sample is being examined now. There are some other conditions that present similar symptoms, so we'll need to check for them, too. Get off the table, turn around, and pull down your pants and underwear."

Tony glanced at his father.

"Would you like me to leave?" Sammy was smiling at Tony's discomfort.

"Would you, please?"

"I'll be outside. Tell me when I can come back in."

As soon as Sammy closed the door behind him, Tony got off the table, slowly turned around, and dropped his pants, completely embarrassed. He stared at a poster of the male and female anatomy on the wall in front of him. He heard Dr. Franconi slip on a pair of rubber gloves.

"What I need to do is massage your prostate. Do you know what that is?"

"I've heard of it."

"It's a gland that surrounds the urethra, by the bladder. I asked you about a discharge before. This will let me see if you have any infection. Lean on the table with one elbow, and hold this at the tip of your penis." He handed Tony a small microscope slide. "Let whatever comes out drip onto that slide."

Tony placed the slide at the tip of what was left of his rapidly receding penis. There was no way he could have anticipated what came next. His feet almost left the ground as Dr. Franconi's finger began to probe for what seemed like an eternity. He tried to concentrate on not dropping the slide, afraid he might have to go through this again. He felt something begin to drip out and managed to catch it. The doctor finished the massage and took the slide from Tony, placed it on a nearby counter, and then removed the gloves, throwing them in a hazardous waste bin.

"One more thing before you pull up your pants. It may be too soon to know anything conclusively, so I want to give you a shot of penicillin, just to be safe. I'll also want to see you again in a month. By then we'll be more sure."

Dr. Franconi left the room and soon returned with a syringe. Tony turned one more time and received the shot.

"That should do it for now," the doctor said. "I'll get your father back in. You can go home. We'll let you know what your specimens show later today."

Tony pulled up his pants. "Okay. Thanks, Doctor."

"You're welcome." Dr. Franconi reached for the doorknob but turned back to Tony before opening the door. "Oh, and in the future, I suggest you use a condom." He smiled at Tony and left.

*   *   *   *

After the appointment, Sammy went home, and Tony went to his afternoon classes. It was better than waiting at home for the doctor to call, and it wouldn't arouse any suspicions with his mother. There was still no news when Tony got home. He went to his room to work on a report, but he had trouble concentrating. He became more worried with each passing minute. At last, the phone rang; someone picked it up during the first ring. He knew his father had it. He ran downstairs to his father's den. Sammy was still on the phone.

"Yes, Doctor. Thank you. I'll let him know."

Sammy hung up and looked at Tony, who was anxiously waiting.

"What'd he say?"

"Looks like you're a lucky man. He doesn't think it's gonorrhea, but he'll give you another test when you see him next month to be sure. He did say you developed a bladder infection, which, coincidentally, showed up now."

"A bladder infection. Did he say how I got it?"

"Could be any number of things. Main thing is, it's probably not the clap. He called in a prescription for some antibiotics at the pharmacy. Go pick it up. I'll give you the money." Sammy took some cash from his wallet and handed it to Tony. "I want the change. Oh, and he said to drink a lot of cranberry juice, so pick some of that up, too."

"That's it?"

"That's it."

Tony started to leave, but turned around. "Listen, Dad. I really want to thank you for helping me out with this, getting the appointment, keeping Mom out of it. It means a lot to me."

Sammy smiled and shook his head. "Actually, I was just relieved to know that you got laid. I was beginning to think you were a fucking queer!"

Chapter 9
July 2003

TRANQUIL MEADOWS WAS a large three-hundred-bed facility. The complex consisted of three wings with two floors in each. The wings served different functions, and specialized staff catered to a variety of residents with short-term rehabilitation needs, more serious medical requirements or Alzheimer's disease, or assisted living care. My father was in the medical section and had the same monitors and I.V.s hooked up to him as he did at St. Luke's.

All the costs for Dad were out-of-pocket once his daily insurance limit had been reached but were less than if my mother had had to pay for St. Luke's in full. Unfortunately, they'd never thought of any long-term-care insurance; and, with no real hope of my father making any attempt to help himself, their savings would quickly disappear. In retrospect, their frugal ways had eventually paid off; there was a good amount to draw from, but it wouldn't last forever.

Tranquil Meadows had a nice dining area that my father refused to use. Since he wasn't moving under his own power, he would have had to be wheeled there, but he didn't want any interaction with the other residents and preferred to have meals delivered to his bed. He barely picked at them anyway, and he was losing weight.

An exercise room was available to the residents, where he could have slowly improved his lung function with some easy activity, but he refused. No amount of cajoling or encouragement from the staff could change his mind.

There was an entertainment room, with a television, games, and scheduled activities designed to improve the residents' quality of life, but Dad was as antisocial as ever and never went there. As usual, all he did was complain. Nobody there did enough for him, and what they did wasn't done right.

On this visit I arrived alone because Kathy and Lisa were attending a bridal shower for one of Lisa's childhood friends. When I walked into the room, I heard my mother from behind the drawn curtain, trying to calm Dad down.

"Sammy, don't get yourself excited."

"The people here are ... useless," he croaked when I got to his side of the room. He needed to catch his breath after every few words.

"What's the problem now?" I asked, sitting in the spare chair.

"Your father's upset because every time they freshen his bed, they take away the extra pillows he wants, and he has to ask for them again."

"These imbeciles ... know I want ... more pillows. How many times ... do I have to ... fuckin' ask them?" His face was getting red, and the veins on his neck were bulging.

"Dad, so ask again. What's the big deal? You're only hurting yourself getting all worked up over a couple of pillows. And how many pillows do you need, anyway?"

"I need two ... for my head. I want one ... under my legs. I want one ... on each side ... for when ... I roll over ... in my sleep."

"Why don't you just sleep in a bed of marshmallows? Don't you think you're being a little ridiculous?"

"I'm paying ... good money ... to be here."

"You wouldn't be paying any money if you'd listened to the doctors right from the beginning. It's your own fault you're here." I was getting steamed.

"Please be quiet, Tony. Mr. Klein will hear," my mother said in a low voice.

"He wasn't in his bed when I walked in."

"He's probably at … the Jew church," Dad said.

"It's a synagogue, not a church," I corrected him, shaking my head. "And that's a building. There's a room here where they hold different religious services. At least he gets out of his bed and does something."

"Where are … the girls?"

"They went to a bridal shower."

"They couldn't … stop here … first?"

"For what? Is something different going to happen today?"

My father closed his eyes, ending the conversation. A nurse walked in. She smiled at my mother and me as she walked to the side of the bed.

"Mr. Giordano, it's time for your bath."

Sammy opened his eyes wide, obviously angry. "Where's my pillows?"

"Excuse me?"

"I never have … all the pillows … I need."

"I'm sorry, I don't know anything about that. Let me take you for your bath, and I'll make sure you have what you need by the time we get back. Would you like to join us, Mrs. Giordano?"

"Okay." My mother looked at me. "Tony?"

"Uhh, no, Mom. I'll wait here. I have no other plans today, anyway."

The nurse helped my father to his wheelchair, and they all left the room. I sat for a few minutes watching television and then remembered I had the *New York Times* in my car. I thought I'd go get it and bring it back to read while I waited. I turned off the television and walked toward the door. As I left the room, I almost bumped into Mr. Klein being wheeled back in. He was in his mid-eighties, I guessed, very thin and mostly bald, with a ring of gray hair circling his head. His eyes were lively, and he smiled when he saw me.

"Hello, Tony."

"Hi, Mr. Klein." I stepped aside and followed as the nurse wheeled him to the side of his bed. When she lifted him to help him get into bed, I gave her a hand. After we got him settled, she made sure he didn't need anything and then left.

"Thanks for helping, Tony."

"No problem. They treating you good here?"

"They're the best. Never have a problem."

"Sounds like you have different people than my father."

"No, they're the same ... oh, I see what you're saying. Yeah, he seems to have more needs than I do, I guess."

"You're being kind. He's always been extremely demanding."

"You were on your way out?"

"I was just getting the paper to read until my father got back from his bath."

"You're welcome to have a seat. I'd enjoy the company, if that's okay with you."

"Sure." I sat in the chair near his bed. "How are you doing?"

"Well, I'm still on the right side of the ground, so that's good."

We laughed. "My father said you were at Jewish services."

"No, no. Pinochle. A few of us get together two or three times a week. Reminds me of my days in the navy. I haven't been to synagogue in ages. I'm an atheist, to be honest. Logic overtook those ancient superstitions a long time ago."

"Well, we have that in common. I was raised Catholic but began doubting when my sister died. It gradually dawned on me that everyone was praying for her, but there really wasn't an invisible man up in the sky who was listening. Eventually I started thinking about all the religions and all the different beliefs and everyone insisting his religion is the true one. My conclusion was that since they can't all be right, none of them are right. And some of these people are ready to kill because they believe their god is better."

Mr. Klein nodded and let me continue. "People just believe in a god because they're taught this stuff as children and don't know enough to question their parents and teachers, and it just keeps getting reinforced. Years ago, when we didn't understand things like thunder and lightning, we created gods who were responsible for those things. And I guess death is a little easier to accept if you believe you're going to be reunited with loved ones in heaven."

"You're preaching to the choir, to use a religious phrase," Mr. Klein said with an impish smirk. "You know what kills me? Politicians have to say 'God bless America' at the end of their speeches, whether they believe or not, because this so-called Christian nation wouldn't accept them otherwise."

"I'm sure they're not all really believers. My mother really hates that I feel this way. I try to convince her I'm right, but she won't hear it."

"Why do you need to convince your mother? If believing makes her feel better, what difference does it make to you?"

"It just bothers me that people hold on to these ridiculous beliefs."

"How do you feel about religions that go out proselytizing and try to convert everybody?"

"They should mind their own business."

"Well, isn't that what you're doing with your mother? Let it go. You're not going to change anyone, and they're not going to change you. If people change, they've got to do it from within, just like you did. If they're curious enough, they'll begin to question and draw their own conclusions. Anyway, what people believe is of no consequence. It's how they act that matters."

"I guess you're right. It's a tough topic to discuss—religion and politics, you know." I changed the subject. "Why are you here, if I may ask?"

"Lupus. Turns out it's not too common in men, but here I am. My wife died three years ago, and we had no children, so I'm better off here. Got to be careful about infections."

"What are they doing for you?"

"Mostly medicating me. I've got a rheumatologist, cardiologist, and kidney doctor seeing me regularly. They're doing what they can. And they have me on a light exercise program."

"What did you do for work?"

"When I retired fifteen years ago, I was the executive VP at Anderson Steel. Heard of it?"

"Sure. I work for North Jersey Tool and Die. We're one of Anderson's customers."

"You're kidding. I know the guy who started that company, Phil Burgess. We used to play golf together."

"Wow. Small world."

We continued to talk as I waited for my father to get back. We covered a lot of ground. He told me about his stint in the navy during World War II, fighting in the Pacific, and how he met his wife, Leah, who was a WAVE. I told him about Kathy and Lisa, whom he had seen during previous visits. He was very easy to talk to and very good-natured, considering his health situation. It was a shame he'd never had any children. I thought he would have been a good father.

When Dad was finally brought back to the room, I got up. "Nice speaking with you, Mr. Klein."

"Please, call me Len. Anytime. I enjoyed your company."

I walked to the other side of the room and watched as the nurse put my father back in the bed. After she left, I said, "Nice and clean now, Dad? Did they get all the important parts?"

"Don't be … an imbecile." He reached for the remote and turned on the television.

"I'm sure glad I waited for you. If you're going to watch TV, I'm going home." I gave my mother a kiss. "Call if you need anything." I turned to my father, who was staring at the television. "I'll see you next week. Try to be more communicative."

I started to walk out, but before I left the room, I heard my father say one last thing to my mother.

"They forgot … the fuckin' pillows … again."

Chapter 10
June 1974

TONY TIED HIS necktie for the third time, hoping he could finally get the front to be longer than the back. His cousin Candace, Luisa and Paulie's daughter, was getting married, and the Giordanos were preparing to go to the wedding.

Tony's abysmal luck with women had left him dateless for this affair, and he would have preferred not to go. His Garbage Truck status from Phi Upsilon Kappa appeared to be continuing, even though he had just graduated from Reynolds University. He received his degree in accounting, which landed him an entry-level position with North Jersey Tool and Die, a small company in town. He hoped this next stage of his life would allow him to meet people who could open up new opportunities for him. With any luck, he might also meet some women and improve his dating prospects.

Anna was going to the wedding with Michael Lambertini, whom she had been seeing for a few months. Clara was happy that Anna had a boyfriend, particularly since he was Italian. Sammy had a different perspective. Mike's hair reached his shoulders, he had a full beard, and he played guitar in a local rock band. Those attributes did not make Sammy happy. The fact that Mike was good to Anna, had an engineering degree, held a good job as a designer at North Jersey Tool and Die, and had helped Tony get his job did not matter.

According to Sammy, Mike was a dirty hippie drug addict, and those goddamn hippies were ruining Sammy's business. Business at the barbershop had been a lot slower since those freaks had stopped getting haircuts.

Sammy and Clara were in their bedroom. "I'd rather have a root canal than go to this wedding," he grumbled, tucking his shirt into his pants.

"Sammy, she's your brother's daughter. Your whole family will be there. You don't see them enough." She turned her back to him. "Could you zip me up?"

"I see them as much as I want to," Sammy said, helping Clara with her dress. "I don't need them any more than they need me."

"Well, it's nice to have a wedding in the family. I was surprised when we got the invitation. Luisa never said anything about Candie dating, and all of a sudden she's getting married."

"He's probably the first guy she ever dated—she's no beauty queen, you know, and a dishrag has more personality. He's either blind or retarded, guaranteed." The ironic parallels to his and Clara's own marriage were lost on Sammy.

"Luisa said they met through work. He's a buyer or something, and her company sells them stuff. That's how they know each other."

"I'm glad to hear you got all the details straight." Sammy mocked her without her realizing it. "Anyway, they'll be saving on electricity, because he's going to want to keep the lights out at night!" Sammy laughed at his own joke.

"Sammy!"

*   *   *   *

The ceremony at St. Andrew's Church seemed interminable to both Sammy and Tony. The old church reflected the generosity of early parishioners, with beautifully ornate stained-glass windows and a large but tasteful marble altar. Delicately crafted statues of several saints, most of whom were unfamiliar to the attendees, kept vigil at the front, as if they were watching for any infractions. What the church lacked was air conditioning, and the hot June afternoon wilted everyone inside. A tall fan stood in each corner of the church, but they just circulated the hot air. Women were fanning their faces with church bulletins but getting no relief.

Sammy kept glancing at Anna and Mike. *Why didn't he have a man's haircut?* he wondered. *What do they do when nobody's watching?* If Sammy ever found out they were having sex, he'd beat the crap out of Mike. *Anna had better wait until she gets married, preferably not to that hippie.*

Tony's mind wandered, too. When they were first escorted to the pew by one of the ushers, he noticed several people, probably in their twenties, who were obviously together, sitting on the groom's side. He kept looking at a girl from that group who was wearing a blue dress. From a distance she looked pretty, with brown hair and a cute smile. Her dress tastefully showed off her figure. She was talking and laughing with everyone, and Tony imagined her having a sparkling personality. He was sure she was with one of the guys in the group. During the ceremony, he couldn't help but glance in her direction every few minutes, hoping to catch her eye, which never happened. What would he do if he did, anyway? *Why can't I meet someone like her?*

*   *   *   *

A ten-minute ride from St. Andrew's took them to the Grand Pavilion, the catering hall where the reception was held. The Grand Pavilion was one of the most luxurious halls in New Jersey, which was no surprise. Uncle Paulie and Aunt Luisa could easily afford it.

"This is setting Paulie back a pretty penny," Sammy said under his breath to Clara as they walked into the expansive lobby. "What's wrong with a VFW hall? This better not give Anna any ideas."

They were immediately directed to a large room for the cocktail hour. Several massive chandeliers illuminated many small tables and plush sofas. Waiters in crisp white shirts and black pants, vests, and bowties stood behind a dozen serving stations that were scattered throughout the room. There were various cheeses and fruits, a carving station with a large roast beef, a table of seafood with an ample supply of shrimp and crab legs, three different pasta dishes at another station, and an open bar.

"Look at this spread," Sammy said. "This is just the cocktail hour, for Christ's sake."

Clara spotted a free table. Sammy and Tony followed her to claim it. Anna and Mike, who were picking up Assunta and Bruno, hadn't arrived yet.

Clara sat and said, "Why don't you two get what you want. I'll hold the table until you get back."

As the men left, Sammy said to Tony, "Don't load up on this shit. Save your appetite for the main course."

"Dad, I think I know how to eat." *Christ, he has to control everything.*

When they returned to the table, Clara got up to get something for herself. Tony's plate was piled high because he didn't want to get up for seconds, knowing Sammy would have something to say. Sammy looked at Tony's plate and shook his head. He and Tony ate in silence until Clara returned.

"I saw Anna and Mike in line by the shrimp cocktail. They found a table on the other side of the room. Mama and Papa are at the table now."

Sammy, who had managed to avoid his in-laws as much as possible since buying his own home, was especially irked at having to spend an evening with them, knowing they'd all be at the same table.

When the cocktail hour was over, the staff opened the large double doors at one end of the room, giving entry to the reception hall, which was set up for three hundred guests. Sammy and his family walked in with the rest of the crowd and found their table. Tony couldn't believe the size of the room, noticing the dais at one end where the wedding party would shortly be sitting. Their table was the second one on the bride's side. As Tony continued scanning the room, he noticed the girl from church. He watched as she and her group sat at a table on the groom's side, farther away from the dais. Tony hoped to position himself at his table to have a view of her, but by the time he was ready to sit, only a chair between his father and Bruno was available, and it faced the wrong way. He sat, hoping to make the best of the next few hours.

The wedding party was announced, and the groomsmen and bridesmaids walked into the hall. They stopped in the middle of the room and formed an arch with their arms. Then the bride and groom were announced: "Mr. and Mrs. Angelo LaPorto." Candace and Angelo walked into the room and under the outstretched arms of their wedding party. Tony hadn't gotten a good look at his cousin in church—he'd been too preoccupied with getting a good look at the girl in the blue dress—but now, as she began her first dance with Angelo, Tony decided she was not as homely as Sammy had made her out to be. He wished he knew her better, that he knew all his cousins better, for that matter, but his father's reclusiveness through the years had kept both Tony and Anna distant from their cousins.

Uncle Paulie got up and, taking a microphone from the bandleader, welcomed the guests. Then the staff brought in the food. As each course arrived, Sammy tried to estimate the bill his brother would be receiving. A Caesar salad was served first, followed by ziti in a Bolognese sauce. Then a lemon sorbet was placed before the guests.

"Dessert, already?" Sammy asked.

"It's to cleanse the palate," Anna said. "You'll be able to taste the next course better."

A server was assigned to each table and informed the guests of their choices for the entrée. "Would you like the filet mignon, chicken Marsala, or grilled salmon?"

Sammy ordered the filet mignon. "I guess that's the most expensive one," he said, leaning toward Clara. "What the hell, Paulie's paying."

Between courses, the band played music from various eras. The rock tunes were much too loud for the older people, who grumbled about it, and the big band-era tunes bored the younger guests, who rolled their eyes at every song. In spite of it all, the dance floor was always filled with people enjoying themselves. They danced to the required Tarantella, Bunny Hop, and Hokey Pokey, which proved that, after several drinks, people didn't know their left feet from their right. Through it all, Tony sat, watching Anna and Mike dancing to everything, wishing he had someone to be with. Occasionally he glanced at the girl and her friends at the table in the back. They were all laughing, having a great time.

At one point, he found himself alone at the table with Sammy. Clara was going from table to table with Nana'Sunta and Bruno, greeting relatives she didn't see as much as she would have liked. Anna and Mike were dancing, and Tony was quietly watching. Out of nowhere, he heard his father chuckle to himself.

"What? Did you tell yourself a joke you never heard before?"

"It's your cousin. I just can't picture Candie with a cock in her mouth." Sammy laughed some more.

Tony knew his father wasn't drunk and looked at him in amazement and disgust.

"Why would you want to?" He shook his head. "I need a drink."

Tony left the table, thinking how crude his father was, and walked to the bar, where a dozen people were in front of him. He looked at the ground.

"This sure is a nice wedding." Tony heard a woman's voice in front of him and looked up.

"Excuse me. My mind was someplace else."

"I said the wedding is very nice. This place is really elegant, isn't it?"

Close up, he didn't recognize her face, but the blue dress was unmistakable. She was prettier than he'd originally thought. It took a few seconds for Tony to compose himself once he realized who she was. He noticed how beautifully her eyes matched her dress, and her soft hair framed her face perfectly.

"Uhh, yeah." Tony could have kicked himself. *What a brilliant response.*

"I saw you in church on the bride's side. How do you know her?"

She noticed me in church? That can't be possible. I wouldn't get noticed if I hit someone on the head with a shovel! Tony thought. Out loud he said, "She's my first cousin, on my father's side. How do you know her?"

"Well, actually, I know Angelo. We work together. There's a group of us from the office at a table way in the back."

"I think I noticed that table. Looks like you're all having a lot of fun."

"We are. It's really a good group. We're all friendly at work; go out to lunch together; sometimes go to happy hours after work. They're all nice people."

The line had been moving up, and the girl was now in front. Tony worked up his courage and made a stab at a joke.

"I'm buying," he told her.

"Thanks. Are you always so generous at an open bar?" She smiled.

They got their drinks, and Tony put two singles in the tip jar.

As they walked away, he knew he had to continue the conversation or else she'd go back to her table. He was never good at this, but he took a breath, and the words flowed—like concrete.

"Uhh, I'm Tony, by the way. I guess I never told you. What's your name?"

"Kathy." She stood for a few seconds, stirring her drink, waiting for Tony to continue the conversation.

"Uhh, are you with anyone? I mean, I know you're with your friends from work at the table and all, but are you *with* any of them?" *Shit, I suck at this!*

"No, we're all just friends." She paused for a few seconds. "And I'm not seeing anyone right now."

"Uhh, would you like to dance?" *Shit, a fast song is playing. I'll look spastic. What am I doing?*

"Sure."

They put their drinks down and walked onto the dance floor. Tony was a wreck. They faced each other, but, shortly after they began to move, the song ended. Tony felt slightly relieved.

"Aww, that was quick," Kathy said, sounding a bit disappointed.

Before Tony could reply, the band began a slow song. Now Tony was starting to sweat. *Do I stay here with her and dance slow? I don't even know her. Is she going to want me to hold her? How do I get out of this?*

Kathy didn't flinch when the song changed. She looked at Tony, sensed his hesitation, placed his right hand behind her back, and lifted his left hand. They began to dance, Tony feeling awkward at first but then comfortably settling in with her. They didn't speak, but Tony could tell she was enjoying herself.

When the song was over, they retrieved their drinks and started walking and talking. They walked through the room where the cocktail hour had been held and into the atrium at the entrance of the Grand Pavilion. They soon found themselves outside and decided to stroll through the gardens that took up a large part of the grounds. Earlier, Candace, Angelo, and their wedding party had used these grounds as a setting for many of their wedding pictures.

"It's nice that it's still pretty light out," Kathy said, glancing at her watch. "It's almost eight thirty." The sun was slowly approaching the horizon.

"Yeah, I like this time of year. As a kid, me and my friends would be outside as long as possible in the summer. My mother was usually the first one to call me in. I used to hate going home when I knew the other guys were still playing."

"My brother Eddie and I were the same. He's older than me, and I guess because he's a boy he tried to stretch his limits with our parents. Didn't always work, though." She laughed. "He definitely got into more trouble than I did."

"How old is he?"

"He's twenty-five, and I'm twenty-one, so there's a few years difference. He's in Connecticut now, works for an insurance company. He got married last year, just before he moved."

Tony's initial jitters had disappeared. He felt like he'd known Kathy for years. They continued walking through the gardens, opening up about themselves. Tony learned that her full name was Kathy Zielinsky. She was a second-generation American; her grandparents came from Poland. Kathy worked as the executive secretary to a vice president of a chain of grocery stores. Angelo was the manager in charge of purchasing produce and reported to the same vice president.

"You mean if I get a mealy apple from a Grand Market store, I can call Angelo and get my money back?" They both laughed.

After a half hour, Kathy said, "I'd better get back to my table. They're going to wonder what happened to me."

"I guess I should, too."

Once they were back in the reception room, Tony realized he had to make an important move, and he had to do it now.

"Kathy, do you think it would be okay if I called you sometime? Maybe do something?"

"Sure, that would be nice."

"Great, I'll give you a call. Thanks for the dance. It was nice getting to know you. Enjoy the rest of the wedding." Tony started walking away, feeling good that he'd gotten the question out without much difficulty.

"Tony?"

He looked back. "Yeah, Kathy?"

"Would it help if I gave you my number?"

Idiot!

"Good idea. Dopey me."

"I think I have paper and a pen in my purse, at the table."

They walked to her table, and she wrote down the information. A few of her friends nodded hello.

Tony took the paper from Kathy. "Thanks. I'll give you a call."

"Okay, Tony. Bye."

"Bye, Kathy." Tony walked away, and in spite of his clumsiness in asking for a date, he felt better than he had in a long time. Unbelievably, he'd met the girl he'd had his eyes on all day.

When he got back to his table, he sat down next to Sammy. Everyone else was there, too.

"Who were you dancing with, Tony?" Anna had a big smile for her brother. "You sure were gone for a long time."

"A girl I met at the bar. Her name is Kathy. She works with Angelo. I may give her a call."

Mike hit the table with his hand a few times. "Go, Tony! She looked cute."

"There must be something wrong with her." Sammy was so encouraging.

Tony just smiled. He almost wanted to thank his father for being an asshole. If Sammy hadn't made that ridiculous comment about Candie, Tony would have probably never met Kathy.

Chapter 11
September–October 2003

THE STAFF AT Tranquil Meadows eventually gave my father all the pillows he had been requesting, but the passing months hadn't changed anything in either his health or his attitude. Rather than being grateful for the pillows and care he was getting, he found other things to complain about. No one came fast enough when he buzzed for a nurse; they gave him a bedpan instead of taking him to the bathroom; they didn't bathe him properly; the staff barber gave him a lousy haircut.

"I could do ... a better job ... on my own head."

"Dad, at this point you couldn't even lift a pair of scissors," I told him. "And you know why? It's because you've been a stubborn ass since you were first admitted to St. Luke's and are a stubborn ass here. Okay, we all know you have COPD, and it's not going away. But you've done nothing in all these months to help yourself. You're lucky you haven't come down with pneumonia. You could've been home a long time ago, with medication and oxygen, doing everything on your own. Now you need someone to wipe your ass."

As usual, he clammed up, which is what he always did when the other person made a valid point that he couldn't refute.

I was the only one visiting on this rainy mid-September Saturday. Lisa was back in school for her final year, and Kathy was home preparing for a girls' night out with some friends. My mother had said she needed to run a few errands, but really she just wanted a break. Her exhaustion was beginning to show on her face. I was afraid her health was going to suffer. Besides the daily grind of driving back and forth to see him, she'd been given her marching orders right from the beginning and still feared she would do something wrong and get chastised for it. He'd never allowed her to make any decisions in the past, believing she was incapable of thinking anything through. Nothing had changed. He made her bring in every piece of mail so he could review it and tell her how to handle it. She would meticulously write his instructions on each envelope: "Send check July 24"; "File with bank statements"; "Throw out." I knew that when she was finally on her own, she'd be leaning on me for any important decision.

I no longer dreaded visiting, however, and was coming to Tranquil Meadows whenever I had the opportunity. It wasn't because I'd suddenly had an epiphany that I didn't know how much longer my father would be around and I wanted to spend as much time as I possibly could with him. I'd never had a minute of quality time with him when I was growing up, and not a minute as an adult, and I didn't care if I spent another minute with him in the future. I started visiting more often because I knew that whenever he decided to sleep or was out of the room for some reason, I'd have a chance to speak some more with Len.

I stopped calling him Mr. Klein after he insisted a few times that I call him Len. Even though I was fifty-one, it was tough getting used to since I'd been raised to address anyone as "Mr." or "Mrs." if they weren't my peer. Since our first conversation had been so enjoyable, I made sure I spoke with him every chance I got. I even took him to the game room a few times when he was playing pinochle, and he taught me the game.

Len always provided a good balance of wise insight and enjoyable small talk. He had an outlook on life that said we should fight battles that were worth fighting but not waste any time or energy on minor things. He said that he and Leah had rarely argued because they were able to overlook the trivial shortcomings we all have that sometimes lead to fights way out of proportion to the original issue.

I knew he and Leah were childless from our first conversation, but I subsequently learned that his wife underwent a complete hysterectomy in her twenties when doctors found numerous cysts on her ovaries and fallopian tube. They never adopted but were able to enjoy children through their nieces and nephews. Len and Leah were able to travel often and always took one or more of the children with them. Even though he never had children of his own, he had a good idea of what fatherhood was like. Now, the children were grown and scattered all over the United States, some in other countries, and he missed them dearly.

Even though I didn't interact with Len while my father was around, on several occasions Dad caught the end of a conversation as he was being wheeled back into the room, or saw me wheeling Len back in after a trip to the game room. He always gave me his patented stare to communicate his displeasure that I was spending time with someone other than him. He never said anything, probably because he figured his message was getting through, but I ignored him and continued spending as much time with Len as possible. I was starting to feel like a cheating husband who was hoping his wife would find out, just to get the marriage over with.

While I was there, Len was taken out of the room for some tests. My father had to get it off his chest, since his quiet hints weren't working.

"You like ... spending time ... with that Jew ... when I'm not here." He had an angry, accusatory expression on his face.

"His name is Len. And you should talk to him once in a while instead of hiding behind this curtain. He's had an interesting life."

"I don't want ... to talk ... to anyone."

"That's been your problem for as long as I can remember. Nobody was ever good enough for your time. You think you know everything and don't want to hear another point of view. You never fully accepted Kathy because she's not Italian. You hated Nana'Sunta and Grandpa because Mom was close to them. I know you were glad when they died within a year of each other and mocked Mom for being as upset as she was."

"Don't get me ... started on them. They hated me ... from before ... your mother and I ... got married."

"All I know is you always holed yourself up in your den. All the friction I ever saw was between you and everyone else, both Mom's family and yours. We hardly ever visited with Uncle Paulie's or Uncle Frank's families, and I barely remember Grandpa Enzo or Grandma Rosa. You were alienated from everyone. You can only blame yourself."

"You don't know ... everything."

"Well, enlighten me."

"You wouldn't ... understand." He paused for a while, as if considering whether he should tell me what I didn't understand. But he changed the subject. "What about ... that Klein, then? What do you ... talk about?"

"It turns out we have a lot in common. Careers, philosophies, interests. He's easy to talk to."

"You never ... had conversations ... like that ... with me."

"You never let me. Anytime I started talking about anything important, you didn't want to hear it. You called me an imbecile and shut me up. You did the same thing with Anna."

"So Klein ... is your ... substitute father?"

"No! He's a friend whose company I happen to enjoy. What? Are you jealous that we have a good relationship?" I already knew the answer but wanted to draw him out.

"When you're here ... I should be ... your main ... concern."

"Then try being civil to me, Kathy, and Mom. Stop being a bastard with the nurses. You know, they always tell us about how you treat them. They're doing their jobs, but they don't need to take crap from you. It's never too late to change. But if you're not around when I'm here, and Len is, I'm going to speak with him."

We talked a while longer, but I may as well have been speaking to the wall. If he had been different from the start, I would have done everything I could to see him through this. But then, if he had been different, he wouldn't have been in this situation in the first place. I decided to leave, with nothing changed.

*   *   *   *

The next time I had a chance to speak with Len, he looked a bit concerned.

"Len, is something wrong? You seem upset."

"I am, Tony. Let me just say this quickly. Your father had a rare conversation with me last week. I guess he didn't tell you, and you and I haven't seen each other since then. He asked a nurse to open the curtain, and when she left, he started talking, which really surprised me. He was straining, but I could hear him. He told me in no uncertain terms that you didn't need two fathers. He didn't like me meddling in your life."

"Meddling? What the—"

"I know it doesn't make any sense, but I don't want to make difficulties between you two. You told me a lot about your relationship with him, and there's no need to make it any worse. You don't know how much longer you'll have him. Maybe you can still salvage something. I don't want to get in the way."

"But you're not. He's just being who he's always been."

"Believe me, someday you'll be happy if you're able to get even a little of the relationship with him you've always wanted. Make the best of what time you have. I'll always appreciate the attention you gave me."

"But this is nuts. He always got his way by intimidating Mom, my sister, and me. Why are you intimidated by him? You're smarter than that and should be able to see right through him."

"Because it's the right thing to do." He held out his hand, and I walked closer and took it. "Thanks, Tony, for all the time you gave me."

"Thank you, Len. I learned a lot from you in a short time. I'll still see you when I visit if you're in the room. At least I can say hello."

"I guess your dad wouldn't object to that." He smiled.

We shook hands and I left. The bastard had won again.

Chapter 12
Anna's Diagnosis 1975–1977

TONY WAS SITTING on his bed reading, his back against the headboard. By August 1975, after a little more than a year at North Jersey Tool and Die, he'd been promoted to accounting manager with three staff accountants reporting to him. He had been seeing Kathy for just as long, and their relationship was progressing nicely. Tony didn't recall ever feeling as completely happy as he was now.

There was a knock at his door. "Tony, can I come in?"

"Sure, sis. I'm decent."

Anna walked in and shut the door behind her.

"What's up, Anna? You look like you're about to burst out of your skin."

"I've got some news, and I want to tell you before I tell Mom and Dad."

Tony moved to the side of the bed, and Anna sat next to him.

"Mike and I have decided to move in together."

"Whoa—that's big! Dad's gonna freak."

"I know. He hates Mike, and I don't think Mom will take it well, either."

"When are you going to move? Where are you going to live?"

"We found a nice little apartment in a two-family house in Nutley. Since I'm going to start teaching in Clifton next month, it's a good mid-point between there and Belleville, where you and Mike work. Mike already put a deposit down. We'll be moving in a couple of weeks. Mike wants to do some painting first."

"That's fantastic. You must feel great finally getting out of here. I'll be happy to help Mike paint or do whatever he needs."

"Thanks. I'm thinking about telling them at dinner tonight. Dad should be home soon. What do you think?"

"That'll make him choke on the *braciole*. But, yeah, you've got to say something soon. Might as well be tonight. You and Mike thinking about getting married, too?"

"We've discussed it, but not just yet."

Tony gave Anna a big hug and kiss. "I love you, Anna. Mike's a great guy, and he's really respected at work. I wouldn't be surprised if he becomes vice president of engineering someday. You two will have a good future. Just tell them as naturally as you can. They may not be happy, but they can't stop you."

*   *   *   *

For the first few minutes of dinner, they sat quietly at the table. Then Anna looked up from her plate and glanced at Tony. He nodded.

"Mom? Dad? I've got something to tell you."

"You better not be pregnant," Sammy said accusingly.

"Dad. Please. No. You know I'm starting a new teaching job next month."

"Yes, sweetheart," said Clara. "It'll be a big change from kindergarten at St. Stephen's. Third grade in a public school will be nice. That's a good age."

"Right, Mom. But you know the school is in Clifton. It's a pretty long commute, when you consider traffic."

"I know, but you live here; what choice do you have?"

"Well," she said, glancing at Tony again. "I'm getting an apartment in Nutley to be closer."

Sammy looked at Clara and then at Anna. "Why would you want to do that? You've got a perfectly nice place to live here, and it doesn't cost you anything. And why Nutley? If you're going to move, why wouldn't it be to Clifton? Nutley doesn't make any sense."

"Well, Nutley is convenient to both Clifton and here."

"I know you'd be close to us and work," said Clara, "but is it really necessary? You're here now, and the commute wouldn't be that bad, really, would it?"

"Well, it's not because Nutley is between my job and here. It's because," Anna said, hesitating. "It's because it's between my job and Mike's job."

"What does Mike's job have to do with it?" Clara was clueless, but Sammy wasn't.

"What are you saying? You're moving in with that hippie?"

"Dad, would you stop calling him that? He cut his hair and shaved his beard months ago. And he's doing really well at work. He's already been promoted to manager of engineering, and according to Tony, there's talk of him being a VP someday."

"I think you should get married before you move in with someone. People will think you're having," Clara lowered her voice, "sex."

"Don't be stupid, Clara," Sammy exploded. "She's obviously already having sex with that loser. How did you raise your daughter? He's going to use her and ruin her for anybody else. Nobody wants someone else's leftovers. He'll knock her up and leave, you watch."

Clara looked at Sammy, shocked. "That's a terrible thing to say."

Anna had years of repressed emotions boiling up. She had never raised her voice to her father and had always tried to keep peace in the family. But enough was enough. She looked directly at Sammy, as angry as she had ever been with him.

"Mike and I love each other, but that's not the only reason I want to live with him. I can't stand living here with you anymore. Ever since I was little, I prayed for the day I would be big enough to leave home. And that's only because of you. I can't take the yelling and screaming anymore. I don't want to put up with the accusations every time I come home from a date, or from anywhere else, for that matter. Am I on drugs? Who was I with? What was I doing? You don't trust anyone. It's like you always expect us to let you down, and you want to stop it before it happens. But you've only pushed me away all these years."

"Anna, please don't yell," Clara begged. "Your father didn't mean what he said, did you, Sammy?"

"Ma, please. Of course he means what he said. I know a lot of what you've been through with him, and I'm sure there's a lot I *don't* know. You have your own reasons for putting up with him, but I don't have to anymore."

With that, Anna pushed away from the table, rose, and walked away. Sammy shouted as she left, "We're not done talking about this."

Anna stopped and turned. "Yes, we are. We're done talking for good." She continued to her room.

Sammy rose, but Clara grabbed his arm and pulled him back into his chair.

"No, Sammy. Please." Tears welled up in her eyes, and she dabbed them with a napkin.

"She'll regret she talked to me like that." The veins in Sammy's neck were popping, but amazingly he remained seated.

Tony was stunned. He was proud of Anna for getting years of unexpressed feelings off her chest, but he knew there would be repercussions.

*   *   *   *

Tony became a frequent visitor to Anna and Mike's apartment. During their first year of living together, Tony was invited to stay on some weekends to get away from his home environment. Kathy and Anna had become very close, and when Tony and Kathy decided to get engaged, they shared the news with Anna and Mike first. They decided on a September 1977 wedding and asked Mike and Anna to be their best man and maid of honor.

Tony's parents had always hoped he would marry an Italian girl. Clara's stance softened once she got to know Kathy, but Sammy, unsurprisingly, never came around. It always seemed that something more than Kathy's ethnicity troubled Sammy, but he never opened up about it. When Sammy and Clara were told of the engagement, Clara was thrilled, but Sammy was cautious.

"How well do you know this girl? Can you trust her?"

"What do you mean? We've been dating for over two years. We know each other very well. Of course I trust her."

"A lot of marriages end up in divorce. You better be sure."

"A lot of people die in car accidents. Should I stop driving? You're being ridiculous. Just because you live your life doubting everything and everybody doesn't mean it's the right way to live."

"If anything goes wrong, don't say I didn't warn you."

"Thanks for the good wishes."

*　　　*　　　*　　　*

Thanksgiving of 1976 was colder than usual in both weather and the atmosphere in the Giordanos' home. The relationship between Sammy and his in-laws remained as strained as ever. Tony had picked his grandparents up early in the day so Assunta could help Clara in the kitchen. Anna was supposed to arrive early to help, too, and that became another sore point with Sammy.

"Anna just called." Clara walked into Sammy's den to give him the news. "She doesn't feel well. She and Mike are staying home."

"My ass, she doesn't feel well. She just doesn't want to spend any time with us."

"No, she's really sick." Clara needed to defend her daughter while not irritating Sammy. "She sounded very weak. She said she's tired and aches all over. She's been feeling worse and worse over the past few weeks. It might be the flu. Would you rather she come and get us all sick?"

"She's faking it, mark my words. That boyfriend of hers is turning her against us."

*　　　*　　　*　　　*

Bruno and Sammy avoided each other's eyes as they sat at the table waiting for Assunta and Clara to serve the first course. Clara's homemade manicotti had been a favorite of Tony's since he was a young boy, and she made it only for holidays. Tony noticed Kathy's eyes darting from Sammy to Bruno; she clearly noticed the tension between the two men. Tony knew this wasn't the first time their frigid relationship was on display for her, but he thought Kathy might have been expecting a thaw for Thanksgiving. He reached for her hand under the table, squeezed it, and looked at her with an impish smile, as if to say, *This is what you're signing up for.*

Clara placed the platter of manicotti on the table and put two on each plate that was passed to her. "I know how much you like these, Tony," she said as she served him. "I'll give you four."

"There won't be much room left for the turkey, but if you insist." Tony hoped the light-hearted exchange with his mother would improve the overall mood, but other than a slight giggle from Kathy, no one gave any reaction.

The family quietly picked at their food as the other courses were brought out. Tony and Kathy finally broke the ice to update everyone on their wedding plans.

"As soon as Anna feels up to it, I want to go with her and the bridesmaids to look at dresses," Kathy said. "There were some pretty ones where I'm getting my gown."

"Anna will be fine tomorrow, I'm sure," Sammy said, his mouth twisted into a skeptical expression.

Clara looked at Sammy and shook her head. "Where is the reception going to be?" Clara asked, turning back to Tony and Kathy. "I know you told me, but I forgot."

"Don Ferrari's out on Route 3," Tony answered. "That's where my company has its Christmas parties."

"Expensive place," Sammy mumbled, shoving some turkey into his mouth.

"It's very nice," said Kathy. "My parents said they'd take care of everything."

"Good for them." Sammy looked down at his plate, unimpressed.

*   *   *   *

By Christmas, Anna still had not regained her strength, and she actually felt weaker than she had a month earlier. She decided to see Dr. Franconi, who managed to squeeze her into his schedule on December 28.

After the nurse took care of all the preliminary checks, Dr.

Franconi joined them. "I haven't felt right in a while," Anna told him. "I can't explain it, but I just want to lie down all the time."

"Your blood pressure is a little low," he said, glancing at Anna's file, "and you look pale. Sandra will draw some blood to help us learn more."

"What do you think it is?"

"It's a little premature to think anything at this point. I don't want to give you any medication until I know what I'm treating. I'll be on top of the lab to make sure we have an answer as soon as possible. Until then, rest if you need to. Try to eat as well as you can to keep your strength up."

When the results were in, Anna asked Clara to come with her to see Dr. Franconi about the findings. Since the Giordanos had been his patients for many years, he saw them in his private office rather than an examination room. The women sat in two guest chairs across from the doctor, who leaned forward from a leather chair behind his large mahogany desk.

After taking a deep breath, he began. "I'm afraid the results were inconclusive. I am going to recommend that you see my colleague from St. Luke's, Dr. Vincent Collins. He's a hematologist and a specialist in blood disorders. From the results I've seen, it appears your white blood cell count is elevated, Anna, but that could mean several things. Dr. Collins can perform additional tests to narrow it down."

Clara looked at Anna and took her hand, gently patting it. Looking back at Dr. Franconi, she asked, "Is it something serious?" Her voice quavered.

Dr. Franconi responded calmly, hoping to ease any premature concerns. "It could be as simple as an allergic reaction or some type of infection, but there are other possibilities, which is why I want to send you to Dr. Collins."

Anna appeared calm. "Whenever I think of a blood problem, I think of leukemia."

"Well, let's not jump the gun. Dr. Collins will be able to be more specific."

Clara tried to compose herself but was already thinking the worst. "Is that possible, Doctor? Could it be leukemia?"

"Like I said, let's not get ahead of ourselves. To be honest, yes, leukemia is a possibility, but it's one of many. Please don't dwell on any potential diagnosis. We simply don't know enough yet." He rose. "Come with me to the front desk. I'll have Carol make an appointment with Dr. Collins for you."

Dr. Franconi escorted Clara and Anna to Carol's desk. After giving Carol his instructions, he extended his hands to Clara and Anna, who each took one. "I'll keep in close contact with Dr. Collins. Please don't worry. You'll be in very good hands."

"Thank you, Doctor," Clara and Anna said in unison. They watched as he turned and walked back down the hallway, grabbed a clipboard from a plastic holder on the wall outside an examination room, flipped through the pages, and prepared to see his next patient.

"He's right, Anna," Clara said, trying to remain calm. "We just have to see what this new doctor finds out."

Carol called Dr. Collins's office while Clara and Anna waited. Carol looked up from the phone, covering the mouthpiece with her hand. "Is Thursday, January 6, at ten o'clock okay?"

Clara looked at Anna, who nodded. "That will be fine," Clara told Carol, who confirmed the appointment and hung up. "Dr. Collins is in the medical building across the street, suite 306." She scribbled the information on the back of Dr. Franconi's card and handed it to Clara. "You'll like him," Carol reassured them. They thanked her and left the office.

*   *   *   *

Clara tried to hide her nervousness as she drove Anna to Dr. Collins's office, although her white knuckles revealed how tightly she was gripping the steering wheel. Snow from a major storm on New Year's Day 1977 still lined the streets. Icy patches from the snow thawing and refreezing made the road more treacherous than Clara was accustomed to. She made every turn with extra care and drove well under the speed limit as fresh snow drifted down. The simple act of Clara driving Anna to the doctor's office in these conditions showed how concerned she was. She normally refused to drive in less than ideal weather, but since Sammy and Tony were at work, Clara needed to overcome her fears. She also felt that as Anna's mother, it was her duty.

Anna was too preoccupied to notice anything different about her mother's demeanor. She silently stared at the road ahead, wondering what to expect from the appointment.

When they arrived at the door to Dr. Collins's suite, Clara immediately noticed the sign outside the office: "Hematology and Oncology." This frightened Clara, but she managed to hide her fear. After signing in and filling out new patient information, they sat down to wait. They both took a magazine from a table in the center of the waiting room and mindlessly leafed through the pages, neither one even noticing what magazine she had picked up. After fifteen minutes, a nurse opened a door and called Anna's name.

In an examination room, Anna sat on the edge of the table and Clara settled into a chair in the corner. The nurse completed her preliminary procedures, and Dr. Collins entered the room shortly after. He was a slightly built man, middle-aged, with graying red hair and a thick mustache to match. He quickly set about putting the two women at ease.

"I know Dr. Franconi told you that there are many possible reasons for your high white blood cell count. We need to narrow down the possibilities and proceed from there."

Anna was quick to respond. "Okay, Doctor. I just want to feel better. I took a leave from my job because I can't get through a day."

"Tell me about your symptoms. What have you noticed?"

"Well, overall, I feel weak. I have very little energy. I ache all over. At first I thought it was the flu and just treated myself with regular medication for flu symptoms, but nothing worked."

"Did you develop a fever?"

"Yes, I still get one. It comes and goes."

"How has your appetite been?"

"Not so good. I've been eating very little. I lost about ten pounds."

"When did you start feeling these symptoms?"

"A few weeks before Thanksgiving."

"So, close to two months, then."

"Yes."

Dr. Collins folded his arms and spoke frankly, his gaze alternating between the two women. "We'll run a few tests. They can be done on an outpatient basis at St. Luke's. First, we'll draw blood for a complete blood count, a CBC, with a blood smear. That will show us different aspects of your blood—red and white blood cells, platelets, and so on. It's more extensive than the blood test you had a few weeks ago. Then we'll do a bone marrow test, where we extract some bone marrow from your hip."

"That sounds painful," Clara said.

"It could be." He looked at Anna. "We'll apply a local anesthetic, but you can also have a sedative to relieve any anxiety you may have. I'll give you a prescription if you'd like."

"I think I would."

As Dr. Collins wrote out a prescription, Anna asked, "After I have the tests, then what?" She became increasingly nervous, constantly shifting her position on the examining table.

"It all depends on the results. We may need to run additional tests, or if we know conclusively what we're dealing with, we'll treat you accordingly. We'll get you in for the tests as soon as possible." He handed her the prescription. "Take this an hour before your procedure. Follow me, and I'll introduce you to Rita. She'll make the arrangements."

"More tests," Anna complained as she and Clara walked out of the office. "We know as little as we did when we walked in."

"He needs to be sure, dear." Clara was just as frustrated but hoped to reassure her daughter. "Before you know it, this will all be behind you."

"I know, but all the doctors, all the tests. I wish it were over now."

They got back in the car and drove home in silence, wondering when the questions would end and the answers begin.

*　　*　　*　　*

Kathy's wedding plans were proceeding nicely. She and Tony worked closely with the event manager at Don Ferrari's, choosing the menu, making seating arrangements, and deciding to use the house photographer. With eight months to spare, the band was booked, the cake and flowers ordered. Kathy wasn't the type to put anything off. She didn't like any loose ends, so she handled everything as quickly as possible. Getting Anna's gown was the only thing left to do. The other bridesmaids had already gone with Kathy to get fitted for their dresses, but Anna never had enough strength. She could barely get through a doctor's appointment, after which she would go back to her apartment to rest. With Mike working, she would often stay at her parents' house so Clara could help with whatever she needed. Sammy never apologized for doubting that Anna was too sick to come for Thanksgiving dinner.

Kathy arranged for a salesperson, Betty, from Bloomfield Bridals, to come to Anna at her parents' house to fit her for her dress. Petite since childhood, Anna had grown into a beautiful and slim young lady, with black hair down to her shoulders. The fifteen pounds she'd recently lost brought her to ninety-eight pounds. Her ribs, shoulder blades, and collarbone were visible as Betty marked and pinned the dress.

"Once I feel better and put some weight back on, I'll be bursting out of this," Anna said, forcing a smile.

"Don't worry about that," Betty replied. "I understand the situation. When the wedding gets closer, we'll make any last-minute adjustments that are necessary. At least the dress will be ordered and altered for now."

"Everything will work out fine, Anna," Kathy said. "You're going to be the most beautiful girl there."

*   *   *   *

Clara drove Anna to St. Luke's three days after first seeing Dr. Collins. Both were nervous about the bone marrow test, but neither one said anything so as not to upset the other. They were taken to one of the rooms designated for outpatient procedures. Dr. Collins and a nurse soon joined them. After some informal greetings and

Anna saying there were no changes to her symptoms, the doctor prepared Anna for what she was about to undergo.

"First, we'll draw a vial of blood for the CBC and blood smear, which will be the same as any other time you may have had blood drawn. For the bone marrow, I want to do two separate procedures while you're here so you don't need to go through this again. You'll be given a local anesthetic, with an injection in your hip, to numb the area." He interrupted himself and looked directly at Anna. "Did you take the sedative I prescribed?"

"Yes."

"Good. I'll do a marrow aspiration first. The needle is thin. It will be injected into the center of your hipbone, and I'll get some of your bone marrow. You'll probably feel a sharp pain while the marrow is being extracted. Once that's done, I'll be performing a trephine biopsy. The needle is a bit thicker than the first one. This will give me a piece of the marrow core. I'll be moving the needle back and forth until I get what I need. You'll feel the pressure and be somewhat uncomfortable, but it shouldn't last long."

Anna was scared but listened quietly and bravely. Clara swallowed hard trying to keep herself from crying. She didn't want Anna to see she was upset. The doctor continued.

"Your hip will be sore for a day or two. I'll give you a prescription to relieve the pain. Are you ready?"

"I guess."

Dr. Collins asked the nurse to draw the blood.

Clara looked away while this was being done and directed her eyes at Dr. Collins.

"How long will it take to get the results?"

"Not too long for the blood tests, but it could be about a week for the bone marrow tests. The marrow needs to be stained to be examined, and that takes a few days."

The nurse completed the blood draw, and Clara left to go to a waiting room. Anna was positioned on her side, and the doctor administered the anesthetic. Moments later the first needle probed into Anna's hip.

*   *   *   *

Everyone was on edge until the results came in. Anna stayed at her parents' house, and Mike joined them each evening. He understood Anna couldn't be alone in their apartment while he was working, and it wouldn't be easy on Clara if she stayed with Anna in the apartment, neglecting her own home.

The call finally came early in the afternoon, exactly one week after the tests. Clara picked up the phone.

"Is this Mrs. Giordano?"

"Yes."

"This is Rita from Dr. Collins's office. Are you and Anna able to see him this afternoon at four? He would like to discuss Anna's test results with you."

Clara stretched the telephone cord from the wall phone to the kitchen table and sat down.

"How is she? What did he find?"

"Dr. Collins will let you know when he sees you. Can you be there?"

"Yes, of course, we'll be there. Thank you." Clara hung up. *If it were good news, Rita could have told me on the phone,* she thought.

*　　*　　*　　*

Clara and Anna arrived just before four o'clock and were taken to Dr. Collins's office. They waited quietly on a small sofa as he rolled the chair from behind his desk and sat directly across from them.

"You know we received the test results, which is why you're here." He took a deep breath. "There's no easy way to tell you this. Anna has acute lymphocytic leukemia. This is normally seen in children, but it's not that unusual for a young adult to develop it."

Both women were jolted by the news and couldn't speak.

"I want to admit her into Blair Cancer Center in New York. It's the finest facility for cancer treatment on the East Coast. I'm also affiliated with them, so I can continue taking care of Anna personally."

"How serious is it, Doctor?" Clara put her arm around Anna and squeezed her shoulder, fighting back tears.

"It appears to be more advanced than the timing of Anna's symptoms indicated." He turned to Anna. "Is there anything unusual you can think about prior to Thanksgiving, beyond the fatigue and aches you had at the time?"

Anna couldn't believe this conversation was about her. She almost felt detached from everything and was slow to respond.

"I'm not sure. This probably isn't related, but …"

"Tell me. Every bit of information we have at this point will be helpful."

"Well, since May or June, my periods have been unpredictable. They always used to come like clockwork."

"That could be significant; it could help pinpoint when this started." He paused. "I know this is difficult, but it's imperative that we begin treatment immediately." He rose and walked to his desk, picked up a few pieces of paper, and handed them to Clara. "Here's some information about Blair, along with directions. It's near the U.N. I'll call and make sure there's a bed for you, Anna. Mrs. Giordano, get her there as early as you can in the morning."

Clara couldn't fight her emotions any longer, and her tears were now flowing freely. "What can you do for her, Doctor?"

"I'm going to start her on a chemotherapy program and also conduct some additional tests to make sure it hasn't spread."

"Am I going to die?" The reality of Anna's situation was beginning to sink in, and fear and shock showed in her face. She, too, began to cry.

"Not if I can help it, Anna." Dr. Collins handed the women a box of tissues. "You'll be in the best place you could possibly be. The staff at Blair is incredible. Everything that can possibly be done will be done." He paused, sensitive to the emotional turmoil they were going through. "Would you like a few moments alone? You can leave whenever you're ready."

"Yes, please, Doctor," replied Clara.

Dr. Collins rose. "I'll stop by and see you at Blair tomorrow, Anna." He left the room.

Clara and Anna looked at each other and embraced, saying nothing.

Chapter 13
The Wedding

CLARA'S NATURAL MEEKNESS evaporated when it came to helping Anna. Waking at five every morning, she made a daily trip from Belleville through the Lincoln Tunnel and across Manhattan. Although only fifteen miles away, it took close to an hour each way, even though she left and returned well before and after rush hour. Tunnel traffic and crossing Manhattan made the trip slow any time of day. Clara was the only one with Anna every day, and she watched her daughter undergo every procedure and treatment she was subjected to.

Sammy made the trip with Clara on Sundays and Mondays when the shop was closed. He would drive on those days, and Clara was glad she didn't have to negotiate the traffic. Feeling bold one morning as they got onto Route 3, heading toward the tunnel, Clara said something that had been on her mind for a while.

"I guess you realize now that when Anna missed Thanksgiving dinner she was already sick. She wasn't avoiding the family."

"Of course, she had to have been sick then. I don't understand what you're saying."

"You thought she was lying about being sick that day. You were very angry."

"You're out of your mind," Sammy said, raising his voice. "I was concerned then, and now I'm very worried about her. I never said anything like that."

"You don't remember telling me she was faking, and that Mike was turning her against us?"

"What? You're imagining things. Don't ever accuse me of that again."

Clara looked away from Sammy and promised to keep her thoughts on the subject to herself. But she knew she was right.

*   *   *   *

The results from the additional tests were not what anyone wanted to hear. A CT scan showed that the cancer had already spread to Anna's lymph nodes. Radiation treatments were added to her chemotherapy. Her hair was slowly falling out, and her weight continued to drop. Through it all, however, Anna was confident she would survive.

"Mom," Anna said one morning in late April as Clara was getting settled in her room, "Kathy called last night, and we talked about the wedding. I can't wait. I'm so happy for her and Tony."

"Yes, sweetheart. All their plans are falling into place. How are you feeling this morning?" Clara pulled a chair close to the bed, carefully avoiding the I.V. tubes and the wires attached to the monitoring equipment.

"Kind of weak. The doctors say it's from all the medication. I'm sure as soon as I don't need them anymore, I'll get my strength back."

Clara, although not as optimistic, said, "I'm sure you will, dear."

*   *   *   *

Through the spring and into the summer, Anna's condition worsened. By early August, she was slipping in and out of consciousness. Her treatment became more aggressive, and Dr. Collins felt the need for a family conference. Except for Assunta and Bruno, who couldn't bear seeing Anna in her condition, everyone attended.

"These last few months have been difficult for all of you, I know."

Dr. Collins spoke to them in a family lounge at Blair. "Anna has been treated with several chemotherapy drugs and intense radiation. The best doctors here at Blair have been watching her closely. She's a fighter. She told me about your upcoming wedding," he said, turning to Tony and Kathy, "and she's determined to be there." He paused and took a deep breath. "You need to understand that may not be possible. She's very weak, and with a month to go before the wedding, most likely she won't have the strength to go."

Sammy was the first to speak. "What are her chances, beyond the wedding date? Is there any hope for her to beat this?"

"Anna is very sick. The cancer has continued to spread in spite of everything we're doing for her. I'm only using the wedding date because that's a big event coming up for the family. I want you to be prepared for anything."

*   *   *   *

Late that night, after returning home from Blair and hearing in his head, again and again, the dire prognosis Dr. Collins had given to the family, Tony lay in his bed, staring at the ceiling. He thought about everything he and Anna had been through together; how they had covered for each other, mainly to avoid any problems with Sammy. They were as close as a brother and sister could be. Sammy had never approved of any of Anna's boyfriends—Mike was no exception—and Tony had always been ready to defy Sammy on Anna's behalf. Many times they would say they were going to a school dance or a movie with a group of friends, only to drop Anna off at a prearranged meeting place to see her boyfriend, and then pick her up on the way home.

Anna helped Tony through many crises, too. When Clara found a small plastic bag filled with marijuana in Tony's room, along with a few packs of Big Bambu rolling papers, she confronted Tony, flushing everything down the toilet while screaming hysterically that her son was a drug addict and threatening to tell Sammy. Fortunately, before Sammy came home from the barbershop, Anna managed to calm Clara down, explaining that a little marijuana didn't make Tony a drug addict and that telling Sammy would create greater problems.

As a result, Tony promised Clara he would never smoke marijuana again and promised Anna he would find a better hiding place.

Tony prayed for his sister, as he'd been taught to in childhood. He asked God how he could allow someone as young and good as Anna to become seriously ill, when many evil people walked the streets. He wanted God to spare Anna and take him instead. He prayed daily, only to see his sister getting worse. It occurred to him that his prayers went no farther than his own consciousness. How was it possible that an invisible man in the sky, there before creation, was actually listening to his and billions of other prayers?

His thoughts returned to this question night after night and expanded into other areas. He questioned the reasons for other injustices that God had supposedly allowed to take place: people starving around the world while others lived in obscene wealth, good people suffering from natural disasters. Why would God allow these things to happen? Did he really control everything that happened? Did he even really know or care what happened on earth? Nothing Tony learned in school and church made sense anymore. The thought of a god actually existing became ludicrous to him. The seeds of doubt had been sown.

*   *   *   *

Tony was in his office at North Jersey Tool and Die three days after the family conference with Dr. Collins. Early in the day, his phone rang. Tony picked it up; his father was on the other end. Sammy never called Tony at work, and Tony instinctively braced himself.

"Son, I think you should come to Blair as soon as you can. Could you call Kathy and Mike and come with them?"

"Sure, Dad. We'll be there as soon as possible. What's happening?"

"Just come."

From that moment, Tony felt as if he were in someone else's body. His head was floating as he robotically got in touch with Kathy and Mike. They agreed to meet at Mike and Anna's apartment and drive into New York together.

*   *   *   *

When Tony, Kathy, and Mike arrived in Anna's room, they found Sammy and Clara seated on either side of her bed. Dr. Collins had been coming and going, consulting with other doctors. Anna was awake and somewhat lucid, drugs relieving her pain. She had become a virtual skeleton in the last month.

"Why don't you sit?" Sammy said as they walked in, rising from his chair. "As long as you're here, Mom and I can take a little break."

As they were leaving, Tony grabbed his father's arm and whispered, "Is this it?"

Sammy said, "Very likely. Dr. Collins suggested we all be here." Sammy took Clara's arm, and they left the room.

Mike motioned for Tony and Kathy to take the two seats. "I don't mind standing." He positioned himself at the foot of the bed, apart from the family, remaining silent as he looked at Anna.

Tony and Kathy each held one of Anna's hands, and she slowly turned her head, glancing at both of them. She managed a smile and gazed at Tony as he rubbed her hand. "I love you, Tony."

He fought back tears. "I love you, too, Anna."

They sat silently until Sammy and Clara returned. Tony and Kathy began to stand, but Sammy motioned for them to remain seated. He stood at the foot of the bed, next to Mike, with Clara at his side. Anna saw her parents walk in. She looked at her mother, and her eyes showed how grateful she was for Clara's constant support. Everyone remained silent for several minutes, until Sammy spoke, addressing Anna.

"Sweetheart, I know I've been tough on you at times." His words came slowly and deliberately. "But I always did what I thought was right. Do you think I've been a good father?"

Tony looked at Kathy with a shocked expression. *How could he be making this about him?*

Anna's eyes went to Clara, who, unseen by Sammy, gave a quick nod. Anna then looked at Sammy and also nodded. Tony couldn't believe what he had just witnessed.

*   *   *   *

Another hour passed, and Anna fell asleep. Everyone took turns staying with her, occasionally allowing the others to take a break and spend some time in the family lounge. Kathy and Clara sat as Tony and Mike paced in the room. Sammy was in the hall, speaking with Dr. Collins.

Kathy heard something and said to Clara, "Did you hear that? It sounded like Anna soiled herself."

"I think I did. Could you find a nurse to help?"

Kathy left the room and stopped when she saw Sammy and Dr. Collins. "Excuse me, Dr. Collins?"

Sammy's back was to Kathy, and he turned, sternly looking at her. "Can't you see we're talking? Wait until we're finished." He turned back to the doctor, who thought it best to see what Kathy wanted.

"That's okay, Mr. Giordano." He looked at Kathy. "What is it?"

"I think Anna just soiled herself. I was going to get a nurse to clean her but thought you would need to know."

Dr. Collins rushed into the room, followed quickly by Sammy and Kathy. By the time they returned, the monitor was buzzing. Clara was standing, in tears, holding Anna's hand. Tony and Mike were on either side of Clara, holding her for support. Dr. Collins went to Anna's side and checked for vital signs. Then he looked at Clara.

"I'm sorry."

"No!" Clara screamed. Sammy put an arm around his wife in an attempt to comfort her. Tony, Kathy, and Mike huddled together, holding one another in support. Two nurses arrived, responding to the signal they'd received from the monitor. The doctor escorted the shaken family to the lounge. "Take whatever time you need in here. You can go back in the room as soon as you're ready after the nurses are done. They'll come for you." He left the room.

Stunned, they looked at one another, tears now flowing freely. Clara repeated, "No! Anna. No!"

"I can't believe she's gone. My big sister, gone." Tony held Kathy tightly.

"Someone needs to call your grandparents," Kathy said. They excused themselves to find a phone so Tony could make a call he'd hoped he would never have to make.

After months of watching Anna's health declining, they had been prepared for the worst, although it didn't make Anna's death any easier for the family to accept. She was twenty-six years old.

*   *   *   *

That evening, everyone in Sammy and Clara's house tried to make sense of the tragedy. Clara and Assunta were crying loudly, screaming Anna's name and alternately shouting "No!" and "Why?" The men unsuccessfully tried to calm them, and eventually Dr. Franconi came to administer sedatives. He stayed to try to give them answers and spoke to Sammy and Tony while the others attempted to comfort Clara and Assunta.

"It was an uphill battle all along. By the time Dr. Collins saw her, the leukemia was already quite advanced, and the cancer had started to spread."

"How does something like that get started?" Tony asked. "Last year at this time, she looked as healthy as ever."

"It's hard to say. It's possible the disease was present all along and something triggered it last year."

"I think I know," Sammy said, glancing over at Mike across the room. "The only thing that's been different recently is that she's been using birth control pills for the past couple of years, ever since she started seeing Mike. There's your trigger."

"I'm not so sure about that, Sammy. I can't say that's totally impossible, but it's doubtful. I haven't seen any literature connecting the two."

Assunta let out a loud wail, and everyone looked her way. "I'd better see to her," the doctor said. He left the two men.

"Maybe he's not sure, but I am," Sammy said to his son. "You'd still have a sister if it wasn't for Mike."

*   *   *   *

Later in the evening, Kathy stepped outside and sat in a chair at the patio table; the house was getting stuffy, and she needed to collect her thoughts. The wedding was only three weeks away, and she thought it might be best to postpone it. She needed to have a serious discussion with Tony, but tonight wasn't the time.

She heard the screen door open and turned to see Sammy walk out onto the patio. Tony had told her about his father's comment concerning Mike and the birth control pills. Her back stiffened when she saw him. She took a deep breath and managed a nod and a comforting smile. Sammy pulled a chair away from the table and sat next to her.

"I can't believe she's gone," he said. They'd never had a one-on-one conversation, and Kathy felt awkward sitting with him, feeling the way she did. Tony's stories about growing up in his household always left her dumbfounded. Kathy had a very close relationship with her parents and couldn't understand the dynamics of Tony's family.

"It's incredibly sad," she replied. "Anna was always so happy, so much fun to be with."

"She was my little girl." He rubbed his eyes.

Kathy couldn't quite gauge the depth of his emotions. She felt his actions were forced and was ashamed of herself for feeling that way. She realized losing a child was the worst fear of any parent, and she had to be wrong. He was always awkward in social situations, and the magnitude of what had just happened amplified his normal discomfort around other people. Sammy must surely be grieving, she thought, but didn't know how to show it.

"I can't begin to imagine what you and Mom are going through. And Nana'Sunta. It's a good thing Dr. Franconi was able to come and take care of them. We've got to watch out for them now."

Sammy reached over and put his hand on Kathy's face, gently rubbing her cheek with his thumb. "I guess I have a new daughter now."

Kathy pulled her head back, slightly shocked by this act of— what? Affection? A cry for attention? She grabbed his forearm and pulled his hand away. Her mind raced to earlier that day, to when Sammy reprimanded her when she came out of Anna's room and asked for Dr. Collins's help. She also remembered his self-centered question about whether he'd been a good father to Anna.

"No. No, I could never replace Anna," she said, trying to be as diplomatic as possible, even though in fact she was repulsed by his touch. "I'll be your daughter-in-law. Nothing more." She pushed her seat back and rose. "Let me see if anybody needs me for anything. I've been gone too long."

Sammy motioned for her to stay, but she pretended she didn't notice. He stared at Kathy as she went back inside, his eyes wide in disbelief at her abrupt departure.

*　　*　　*　　*

Kathy waited until the evening of the funeral to speak with Tony about their wedding. The three days after Anna died had been a blur. The wake and funeral were a testament to how much Anna was loved. Friends from throughout her life came to say their final goodbyes, including many of the parents from her third-grade class. Tony made sure his mother and grandmother took the medication Dr. Franconi prescribed, but that still didn't prevent them from throwing themselves on the casket in the funeral home and wailing loudly during the services.

Now, with the wedding only two weeks away, a decision had to be made. The night of the funeral, after Clara and Sammy had gone to bed, Tony and Kathy held each other on the sofa in the quiet living room.

"Tony, we need to talk about the wedding."

"It's going to be surreal. I don't know what to expect from my mother and Nana'Sunta."

"That's what I want to talk about. I don't think they, or most of your family, for that matter, will be ready to celebrate a wedding so close to Anna's funeral."

"What can we do at this point? I mean, everything's in place."

"Postpone it. It can be done. We'll just cancel the flowers and the cake. Those things aren't ready until the last minute, anyway. They can hold our deposit until we have a new date. The reception will be trickier. My parents may lose their deposit unless Don Ferrari books something else, which is unlikely with two weeks to go. But they're prepared for that. I already mentioned the possibility to them."

"No. I don't think postponing the wedding is necessary. You're right. It'll be tough for my family. I'm sure it'll be hard to switch their emotions so soon; it's going to be tough for me. But I think a happy occasion would be helpful. We've got to try to get our lives back to normal. Our wedding could be the first step in that direction."

"Are you sure? I don't want anyone to think we don't care about Anna's memory."

"Nobody will think that. Don't worry. Everyone will be happy for us."

*   *   *   *

The wedding went on as planned. Kathy looked beautiful in her gown, and Tony made a handsome groom. Mike still agreed to be Tony's best man, and one of Kathy's cousins, who'd originally been a bridesmaid, served as her maid of honor. A coworker from Kathy's office was gracious enough to even out the wedding party on short notice. It hadn't occurred to her—or maybe she didn't mind—that she was wearing the dress originally meant for Anna, which the bridal store altered at the last minute.

The church ceremony was particularly touching, as the priest, a longtime friend of the family, made reference to Anna during his sermon. Kathy's parents, although not wealthy, proved to be marvelous hosts and gave her as elegant a wedding as they could afford. Don Ferrari's pushed their budget as far as possible, and the cocktail hour, reception, and the wonderful desserts on the Viennese table were all well received.

The Zielinskys hired a Polish wedding band that had performed at many of their friends' affairs. Tony and Kathy were surprised to hear their first song, "Time in a Bottle," played in a polka style, which provided one of the few laughs of the night. Beyond that, there was little genuine joy from the crowd, given the circumstances.

A month later, as Tony and Kathy looked through the proofs, trying to choose the photographs to include in their wedding album, they couldn't find even one that showed a smile on either Clara's or Nana'Sunta's face. The one of Tony and his mother dancing showed a completely joyless woman. Nothing could have made her smile so close to the tragedy of losing Anna, and the pain would never completely leave her. That void existed in Clara's heart every day.

*　　*　　*　　*

Mike eventually lost contact with the Giordanos. He left North Jersey Tool and Die two years after Anna died, moved to North Carolina, and started an engineering consulting company. The last Tony had heard, Mike's business was doing very well; he married and had a son. Tony believed that Anna and the hippie would have had a good life together.

Chapter 14
November 2003

WITH NO MEANINGFUL conversations with Len Klein to look forward to, I had no reason to visit my father any more than I felt was necessary. Surprisingly, my mother, who had been at my father's bedside virtually all her waking hours since he was first admitted to St. Luke's, also cut back on the time she spent with him. She skipped many days altogether, and when she did decide to show up, it was for only a few hours. My mother was getting used to living alone, and I could sense she enjoyed it. For the first time since she had married my father, Mom had control over her own life.

"I hate to say it," my mother told Kathy and me one evening when she came to our house for dinner, "but I enjoy the quiet. I'm not walking on eggshells, worrying if I said the wrong thing or if I'm not doing something right."

"Mom, why couldn't you ever put him in his place?" Kathy asked. "If Tony ever tried half of what Dad did, I'd make sure he knew about it."

"She's not kidding, Ma!" I laughed.

"I don't know. I guess it's a lot of things. You know our marriage was arranged, don't you, Kathy?"

"Yes, Tony told me."

"Nana'Sunta kept me very sheltered when I was growing up.

At the time it made me feel good; made me feel loved. And I'm sure Nana had the best of intentions. But my world was very small."

"You never rebelled to get some freedom?"

"No. I guess I liked being taken care of. I never did well in school. I left school in the middle of the eighth grade, when I was sixteen. I got left back a few times. I never went to high school. I got a job where Nana worked. I was a seamstress in a coat factory, doing piecework. It was the only job I ever had. When my Uncle Carmine told Grandpa about this young man who was working for him and wanted to come to America, things just fell into place. Daddy was able to provide for me right away, and when Anna came along, I never had another job, not that Daddy would have allowed it.

"He left once for a few days. We had a big blow up. Do you remember, Tony? Anyway, he returned, and I took him back, because I didn't know how I would have functioned alone."

"I remember. Anna and I were kind of glad he left and were disappointed when he came back. But you had Nana'Sunta and Grandpa to help you with Anna and me. You could have functioned."

"Not as well financially. Daddy always was a good provider. I know we were never extravagant, but you and Anna always had what you needed. I never thought about alimony and child support at the time. Maybe we could have done okay. But besides that, there was the stigma of having a broken marriage. It just wasn't done then, at least not in our family. I wouldn't have been able to face anybody."

"Everyone knew the kind of husband and father he was; they would have understood."

"Maybe, but forty years later that's easy to say. I made a decision then and there to keep the family together, right or wrong."

"I had my share of problems with him, too. I know that's no secret," I said. "I hated that he made me shine shoes in his shop from when I was nine years old. I did that for years. He thought I was too shy and wanted me to interact with people. He ruined my Saturdays and summers. I used to pray that people walked in with sneakers or sandals so I wouldn't have to walk up to them and say 'Shine, sir?'

the way Dad instructed me. I was mortified. I wanted to just sit in the corner of the shop with my Hardy Boys book."

"You were kind of quiet when you were little. It probably did you some good."

"I'd rather have been playing in Little League, like a normal kid. And do you remember when he chased me up the stairs with the fireplace poker?"

"What?" Kathy asked.

"I guess I never told you. I forget now why it happened. I'm sure I just talked back to him. I was about sixteen. He grabbed the poker and chased me upstairs."

"You called him a hypocrite because he was always making us go to church," my mother reminded me, "but you felt he didn't act like a good Catholic the rest of the week. And don't leave out the part that I got myself between you two and blocked him on the way up the stairs," she added.

"Oh, yeah, that's right," I said sheepishly. "I guess you saved my sorry ass."

"I did that more times than I care to remember."

"Well," I said, "it's all water under the bridge now. Let's have some of Kathy's terrific blueberry pie!"

*　　*　　*　　*

The last few times I visited my father, I noticed that Len was looking thinner than usual; his face was gaunt. I never had an opportunity to ask how he was; I could only nod and smile as I walked to my father's side of the room. When I arrived this time, Len was not in his bed.

My father also looked weaker, laboring for breath more than ever. Now, at least, it made sense for him to be uncommunicative, but when he had something to say, he made sure he got his message across.

"You should ... all be ... ashamed of ... yourselves." His bed was at a forty-five-degree angle, with pillows all placed as per his directions. His eyes were wide in anger.

"What are you talking about now?" I asked. I was alone with him, my mother enjoying a Sammy-less day.

"None of you … including … your mother … show any respect … for me."

"What do you mean?" *Let the bastard talk*, I thought. *Waste your breath on this nonsense.*

"All I've done … over the years … for all of you … and you … let me … lie here … alone … every day."

"What you've done is ruin your life, and ours, by your own actions. Do you really expect sympathy from me or anyone else when you're here because of your own stubbornness? And you expect respect? How can we respect anyone who's too stupid and stubborn to take care of himself? You deserve your situation right now."

"Watch your tongue … don't forget … I'm your father."

"Maybe that's what my birth certificate says, but my experience says otherwise. You've demanded respect from everyone for as long as I can remember, but what have you ever done to earn it?"

He hesitated, and his eyes, opened wide, looked even more enraged. "I should have … jerked off … the night … you were … conceived."

I stared at him in amazement. "Twisting the knife is what you do best, isn't it? I remember years ago when you left for a few days. Anna and I were upset for Mom, but happy that we might never have to see you again. Then you came back and ruined everything. The only reason Mom took you back was for money, not love. We all would have been better off if you'd stayed away forever."

Just then there was a sound of a wheelchair coming back into the room. I didn't want Len to hear any of this, so I stopped speaking. My father saw me glance back at the curtain as I listened to the nurse getting Len back into bed.

"There you are, Mr. O'Hara. Can I get you anything?"

"No, missy. I'm fine, thanks."

I heard the nurse leave and looked at my father, who had a wicked smile on his face. I left his bedside and walked around the curtain to the other side of the room. I didn't recognize the man in the bed, and I guess my face showed confusion and shock.

"Something wrong?" the man asked.

I left the room without answering and looked at the nameplates at the door. Kenneth O'Hara was where Leonard Klein used to be. *Why hadn't I noticed this before? How long has O'Hara been in this room?* I walked briskly to the nurses' station and found a male nurse entering data into a computer.

"Excuse me, can I ask you a question?"

"Sure."

"My father, Savino Giordano in 215, had a roommate, Leonard Klein. I haven't been here in a while. Was he released?"

"No, sir, I'm afraid Mr. Klein passed away earlier this week."

I was stunned. "What? How?"

"His condition worsened over the last month, and his heart gave out."

I walked away from the nurses' station in a fog. In total, Len and I had spent but a few hours together, in conversation or enjoying the game room with other residents, but I felt I'd really gotten to know him. I would have known him even better if my father hadn't intervened. My father. He knew Len had died. I could tell by the look he gave me when I learned Mr. O'Hara was in that bed. He wasn't going to tell me. I walked back into the room, quickly passing Mr. O'Hara's bed, and walked right up to my father. I had no idea how loud I got, and I didn't care.

"You knew about Len, didn't you? You were happy when I found out."

"Why should ... you care ... about that ... old Jew?"

"You hate everyone, don't you? What are you going to do if I get friendly with Mr. O'Hara? Ask me why I would talk with an old mick? Leonard Klein was a good man. I wish I knew him better, but I guess you were afraid I would see what I might have been missing all my life. You'll get what you deserve someday."

I turned and stormed out of the room. From the corner of my eye I could see poor Mr. O'Hara watching me, probably wondering why his name got mentioned in our argument and planning to ask for a room change.

I got into my car and started it, still fuming at my father and thinking about Len. I couldn't put the car in gear—I wasn't ready to drive. I thought about some of the conversations Len and I had had, how he'd been able to put life in perspective. I remembered when he taught me how to play pinochle with his friends in the game room. I wished I could have said goodbye. I put my hands at the top of the steering wheel and placed my face between them. I began to cry, a little at first and then uncontrollably. Eventually I regained my composure and managed to drive away. In spite of all his wisdom, Leonard Klein was wrong about one thing. There was no hope of salvaging any sort of relationship with my father.

Chapter 15
Naples–1932

THE WORLDWIDE DEPRESSION was felt in Italy in the same devastating way as it was in every economy. Using worthless currency, banks took over the assets of many failed industries, and the financial institutions soon followed them into bankruptcy. The government stepped in, creating several agencies to prop up the troubled businesses, but it wouldn't be until the 1950s that the economy turned around enough to resemble pre-depression conditions.

Enzo Giordano was positioned to take advantage of this environment. As a low-level enforcer for Giorgio Manetti, don of the Naples Camorra, he made a living by arranging loans for individuals and shopkeepers caught in a tight monetary squeeze and collecting their weekly payments. Manetti gave Enzo a percentage of the take, but occasionally Enzo was able to set a loan at a higher rate than Manetti authorized, and he kept the difference for himself—a dangerous but profitable risk he was willing to take. As Enzo traveled throughout the Campania region in his beat-up Fiat 509, his first business transaction at every location was to secure the services of a local lady. Word would never get back to his wife, Rosa—not that he cared if it did.

The Giordanos' home was in the Arenella quarter of Naples, a sparsely populated neighborhood set on the Vomero hill above the city. Enzo had inherited the house from his parents. It was secluded and surrounded by woods, as far away from other people as one could get in Naples.

*   *   *   *

Enzo threw a few items into his valise and walked into the kitchen, where Rosa was preparing dinner. At forty, he was thin and wiry, with a heavy black moustache. "I'm leaving for a few days."

"Where are you going?" Rosa asked, knowingly overstepping her bounds.

"You don't need to know. I have business to take care of."

Rosa wiped her hands on her apron. "When will you be back?"

Enzo put his valise on the table. "When I'm done. Why are you asking these questions? My business is not your concern."

"Enzo, why must you keep secrets from me? The boys never know where their father is. They ask questions, and I don't know what to tell them."

"Why would they care? Do you have food to eat? A roof over your heads? That's all you need to know."

"You always come and go with no explanation. I feel like I don't know who you are."

Enzo's right hand came from nowhere and slapped Rosa's face hard. "That's who I am. Leave if you don't like it. You've got nowhere to go. Maybe you'll learn to shut your mouth." He grabbed his valise and walked out of the house.

Rosa sat at the kitchen table, sobbing and rubbing her cheek. At thirty-eight, after eighteen years of marriage, she'd never been told how Enzo earned a living and rarely questioned him. She should have known better than to challenge him. Savino, who had been watching secretly, ran back to the bedroom he shared with his brothers, instinctively realizing his mother would be humiliated if she knew he had seen what happened. At ten, Savino was the youngest of the three boys, and he had seen this behavior from his father many times before. Enzo didn't care if his sons witnessed his actions, and they all had both seen and been victims of his rage. He liked being feared; fear brought respect. Enzo's temper was quick, and no one wanted to be on the wrong end of it.

* * * *

Savino, Paolo, and Franco were never close growing up. Savino was the youngest by six years due to several miscarriages and the deaths of two infant siblings. Paolo was the oldest at seventeen, and Franco was sixteen. Savino was always at a disadvantage because of his age, and his brothers constantly tormented him and laughed at his every shortcoming.

Enzo didn't believe in giving his sons a formal education. The boys went to school just long enough to learn how to read and receive basic math skills. By thirteen, they were done with their studies and sent to work. Savino was still in school, but Paolo, who planned to open a grocery store as soon as he saved enough, worked at a vegetable cannery. Franco apprenticed as a carpenter. His older brothers constantly reminded Savino that he was the baby in the family and not carrying his weight.

"Savino, when are you going to bring some money into this house? Maybe you shouldn't eat until you can pay for your own food." This was one of many taunts Savino heard on a regular basis.

"When you were my age, you didn't make any money. Leave me alone."

The gap in their ages was the obvious reason Savino became their target so often; the older brothers were constantly strutting around, displaying their natural machismo, which Savino lacked at his age. In addition, Enzo encouraged rivalry among the boys, believing that fighting for everything they got would make them men.

Both Paolo and Franco would slap Savino in the back of his head, calling him an imbecile. They pushed him around for no reason, making sure he knew their superiority. Once, under the pretense of playing a game with Savino, Paolo and Franco blindfolded him, put him in a wheelbarrow, and took him deep into the woods. They told him a surprise was out there. They tilted the wheelbarrow, spilling Savino onto the ground, and then grabbed him, shoved him against a tree, and tied him to it. They ran away, listening to him crying and screaming to be let go. At dinner a few hours later, the older boys, who obviously hadn't thought through their scheme, denied knowing where Savino was, but Enzo beat it out of them. Enzo went with them to free Savino, who also got a beating for being stupid enough to be put in that situation.

Unable to take the constant abuse, Savino ran for solace to the only friend he had. Rigoletto was a dog of undetermined mix, about the size of a German Shepherd, with short hair and a friendly disposition. He had limped onto the Giordanos' property twelve years earlier, when Paolo was five and Franco four. The dog favored his left foreleg, and his back was slightly deformed. No one in the family remembered seeing him in the area, and there was no way to know if he belonged to someone. Most likely he'd been abandoned due to his condition. The boys wanted to keep him in spite of his physical shortcomings, and Enzo allowed it, as long as he stayed outdoors. Rosa gave him his name, after the hunchbacked character in the opera, and helped Paolo and Franco make a home for him under the stairs leading to the rear entrance of the house.

One of Rosa's few pleasures was watching her boys play with Rigoletto. Every so often she would take her 35mm Leica camera and take some photographs. Enzo had received the camera from a shopkeeper whom he had uncharacteristically helped when the man fell short on a payment. Enzo had no use for it, but Rosa had always wanted one, so he took it.

When Savino was eight years old, Rosa watched him from the kitchen window as he played and rolled on the ground with the dog. She took the camera and walked outside.

"Savino, stay still and hold Rigoletto. I want to take a picture of you."

Savino stopped and grabbed the dog, getting ready to pose. Just before Rosa could snap the picture, Savino waved his hands.

"Wait. Not here. Follow me."

Savino started running into the woods, Rigoletto following him and Rosa walking behind, wondering where they were going. Savino stopped in front of a large old oak tree, about a quarter mile into the woods.

"This is our tree. It's where Rigoletto and I think. Take our picture here."

Rosa laughed. "If that's what you want."

Savino knelt next to Rigoletto and hugged him around his neck. Rosa snapped their picture. "That's a good one, Savino. Time to go back."

*   *   *   *

Eventually, Paolo and Franco grew tired of Rigoletto, and Savino took over his care. The dog became older and feebler, but Savino's love for him grew. Just as Rigoletto must have felt before he was taken in, Savino believed he was unwanted in his own home. His brothers were relentless in their teasing. Rosa, weary from her responsibilities in the house—raising three boys over the past sixteen years—and Enzo's cruelty, gradually gave Savino less attention. And he lived in fear of Enzo.

One morning, Savino called out to Rigoletto as he stepped out of the house.

"Rigo, come."

Savino ran away from the house and into the woods, Rigoletto limping behind him. They stopped at the oak tree, Savino's special place. It wasn't as far in as the one that had once held him prisoner. He sat under the tree and reached out for Rigoletto when he caught up. The dog licked Savino's face enthusiastically, and Savino hugged him tightly.

"You're my only friend, Rigo. Paolo and Franco hate me. Papa is mean to everyone, and Mama doesn't care. I have no friends at school. Someday, Rigo, you and I are going to run away and start a new life far, far from here."

Rigoletto continued licking Savino's face. "I love you, too, Rigo. Someday … someday."

*   *   *   *

Enzo sat on an old chair outside the back door of the house. It was early fall in 1932, and a cool, comfortable breeze provided a rare, calming respite for him. He whittled a thick branch that had fallen from a nearby pine tree, occasionally inhaling smoke from a cheroot that dangled loosely from his lips. As he mindlessly performed this activity, he saw Rigoletto rolling vigorously on a patch of grass and vomiting. Enzo dropped his knife and stick and slowly walked over to the sick dog. As Enzo carefully inched nearer, Rigoletto collapsed on his side, panting heavily. *The dog is old,* thought Enzo. He squatted down and looked at the dog more closely. Rigoletto's eyes were open, but they gave him only a vacant stare. Enzo rose and walked into the house. A moment later he came back out, entered a nearby shed, and emerged with a shovel. When he returned to Rigoletto's side, the dog seemed more alert, and Enzo managed to get him on his feet. "Come, Rigo." He grabbed the dog by the scruff of his neck and lightly pulled to get Rigoletto to follow him.

"Where are you going with Rigo, Papa?" Savino came out of the house at the wrong time.

"Go back inside, Savino." Enzo looked sternly at his son and then continued walking into the woods with Rigoletto, the shovel propped on his right shoulder.

Savino knew he was expected to obey his father without question, but as Enzo entered the woods, Savino ran behind, keeping a safe distance and hiding behind trees as he proceeded.

A few minutes later, Enzo and Rigoletto came to a halt near Savino's oak tree. His father didn't know the tree was special—it was simply a good spot. Savino peered around a tree and quietly watched as Enzo put the shovel on the ground and bent over to stroke Rigoletto's deformed back a few times. Then he got up and in one motion reached into his right jacket pocket, pulled out a pistol, and shot Rigoletto in the head, the dog dropping instantly. Savino let out a scream and ran from behind the tree. "Rigo! No! Rigo!"

Savino knelt next to Rigoletto and hugged him tightly, crying. He watched the blood flow from Rigoletto's head.

"What are you doing here? I told you to stay in the house."

Savino didn't reply. He held Rigoletto as he sobbed and tried to catch his breath.

"Be a man, Savino." Enzo was impatient with his son's display of emotion. "It's just a dog. Men don't get overcome by their emotions. They deal with things sensibly. As long as you're here, you can help me bury him." He bent down and picked up the shovel, extending it out to Savino. "Dig."

Savino rose, still crying, and took the shovel from his father. Slowly, he dug a hole, weeping the whole time.

"Stop being a baby. Rigoletto was old and sick. He was on his way out, anyway."

*   *   *   *

That night, Savino lay in bed, thinking about Rigoletto. He was more determined than ever to leave the house as soon as he was old enough. Now it would have to be without Rigoletto, his only friend. The memory of watching his father shoot him would remain with Savino forever. No dog would ever replace him.

Chapter 16
Corsica–September 1943

*S*AVINO WAS DRAFTED into the Italian army in November 1942. Although he'd been forced to leave his job at Carmine Esposito's barbershop, he was actually enjoying his military service. At twenty-one, Savino still felt uncomfortable in his own home. Paolo and Franco were also in the army, serving in North Africa and the Balkans, respectively, but until they left home they'd still managed to make life for their younger brother unbearable. By the time they began their military service, Savino's older brothers had their own businesses; Paolo owned a small grocery store, and Franco made high-quality furniture and cabinets. Savino, working for someone else, still wasn't successful enough in his brothers' eyes.

When his training was complete, Savino joined the occupying forces in Corsica, stationed in a small village outside Bastia, a coastal city in the northeast. Since Savino's arrival, the occupation had been uneventful. Savino knew he was very fortunate not to have seen combat so far. Since he'd come ashore in January, his duties primarily consisted of being the captain's personal chauffeur and the division's barber.

Driving one of the company's staff cars, a Fiat 508c Militare, Savino would regularly drop off Captain Alfonso DiLauro at his temporary headquarters, in the mayor's house. He would then drive back to the makeshift barracks the Friuli division now called home.

*　　*　　*　　*

In the army, Savino finally felt like he belonged. He was close to his comrades, seeing them regularly as he kept their hair shorn close to their scalps. One soldier in particular, Pietro Cavalla, became Savino's confidant. Pietro had been a sous chef at a restaurant in Taormina, in Sicily, and hoped to open his own restaurant when the war was over. He had piercing dark eyes and a cocksure attitude that bordered on arrogance but was tempered by his charm. He was the same age as Savino, who found him easy to talk to; Savino wished he had a brother like him. The two soldiers had endless conversations about their futures.

"Savino, you have to come to Taormina when we get out of this shit-hole army. We'll be partners. I'll have the best restaurant in the city," Pietro said as they walked through the barracks, taking time to have a smoke.

"I'm a barber. What do you expect me to do in a restaurant?" He lit a fresh cigarette with the butt of another.

Pietro slapped Savino on the back. "You're smart. You can learn. I'll be in the kitchen. You'll be up front. You can be the maître d'."

"I don't know," replied Savino, inhaling the smoke deeply. "I'd like to leave Naples, though. I've heard Taormina is beautiful."

"Do it. You'll love Taormina. We'll have a wonderful partnership. You know what you'll love best?"

"What?"

"The women. They're the most beautiful women in Italy. You'll be surrounded by them."

"You know I have my eyes on Colette."

"That's because you're here. You don't really think that will lead anywhere, do you? And besides, she's the enemy. If you get caught fraternizing …"

"Don't say anything. You're the only one who knows."

"You know I would never betray your trust."

*　　*　　*　　*

Colette Poggi was the main reason Savino looked forward to transporting Captain DiLauro to and from the mayor's house. Colette was Mayor Gaston Poggi's daughter. He was a widower and had raised her on his own since she was three. At nineteen, she had long black hair, a slim figure, and a face as beautiful as any Savino had ever seen. Savino loved to stare into her wide, curious black eyes while they had their many conversations in the mayor's library or in the staff car; on free evenings, they would drive to a secluded spot about a mile away.

On many occasions, Savino would wait in the mayor's large library while the captain and the mayor were presumably discussing something important behind closed doors in the mayor's office. Savino enjoyed waiting because it gave him a chance to admire the various stringed instruments the mayor had on display. A few rested on special holders, either hanging from the walls or leaning in a corner of the room. The collection included guitars, mandolins, violins, and other instruments that Savino couldn't identify. Several were in what Savino believed to be specially designed cabinets that the mayor kept locked.

Colette walked into the library one day, surprising Savino as he walked from one instrument to the next.

"Do you like them?" she asked, quietly approaching him from behind.

Savino jumped and turned around. "You startled me. Yes, he has quite a collection. I don't know what half of them are, but I assume they're quite valuable."

"A few are antiques. That violin over there is a Stradivarius," she said, pointing to a shelf in one of the cabinets. "Papa has been collecting them for a long time. A few are valuable, but most of them have no special significance. Some of the local businessmen give them to my father as gifts, usually when they want some kind of political favor."

"I never learned how to play an instrument, but I always loved music and admire people who have the talent to play."

Colette looked at Savino for a few moments and smiled. "Would you like one?"

"What? How could I take one? Your father would notice immediately, I'm sure."

"Wait here."

Colette left the library and walked up the stairs. In a few moments she returned with an unusual-looking instrument.

"What is that?"

"This is called a cittern. Papa taught me a lot about his collection. An attorney who has passed away gave this to him years ago. There is no chance of him visiting, so it is never on display. Take it."

"I can't. We should ask him first."

"Trust me. It's been sitting in a spare room upstairs with a dozen other instruments. He'll neither know nor care that it's missing."

Colette held it out for him to take. He looked from the cittern to Colette and back again.

"You're sure?"

"Please. Take it. Then you'll have something to remind you of me."

"I'm hoping I won't need an object to remember you by; you know that." He paused for a moment and took the cittern. "Thank you. As long as you're in a generous mood, can I ask for something else?"

"That depends. What?"

"Do you have a photograph of yourself that I could have? That way I'll be able to see you when we're not together."

Colette giggled. "You want a picture of me? I'm honored. I think I have one to give you." She ran back upstairs and quickly returned. Handing a photograph to Savino, she said, "Papa took this of me standing in front of the church on Easter this year. I don't need to look at myself. You can have it."

Savino looked at the photo. "You look beautiful. But of course you do. You *are* beautiful. Thank you." He gave her a quick kiss. "Let me put these in the car before the captain comes out." He ran out to the car and put the cittern and the photo in the backseat, covering them with a blanket, and then went back into the house to wait for the captain. Colette excused herself, and Savino watched her as she ascended the stairs, admiring her every step.

*   *   *   *

One night, after bringing the captain back to retire for the evening, Savino lingered in the staff car. Colette soon came out of the house, and they drove to their spot. He stopped the car and turned to look at her. With only the moonlight to illuminate them and no one nearby, Savino put his arm around Colette's shoulder and drew her closer. He gave her a long, deep kiss.

"Do you know how much I love you?" He looked directly into her eyes.

Colette giggled. "You tell me every time we're together. How could I not know?"

"You still haven't answered me. I've asked you so many times. Will you come to Italy when the war is over and marry me?"

"There is so much that can happen before this war ends. I enjoy your company. We should wait and see what happens."

Savino leaned in for a kiss, and his left hand explored between Colette's legs. She gently grabbed his wrist and pulled his hand away.

"No. It's too dangerous. Don't forget, I'm the enemy. Your captain makes sure my father remembers that every day, even though he's cooperated from the beginning."

"No one will see us. And what's the difference? Just sitting here with you would be bad enough. Why can't we show each other how much we're in love?"

"No. I don't want it on my conscience if we're caught and you get in trouble."

Savino turned away and leaned back in his seat. "It's so difficult loving you so much but not loving you totally."

Colette put her hands on his cheeks. "You look so sad." She kissed him and then unbuttoned her blouse to the waist, exposing her petite breasts. She put her hands behind his head and pulled him into her chest. Savino kissed her breasts for the first time. He fondled them and licked her hardened nipples. Then Colette abruptly pushed his head away.

"No more." She buttoned her blouse. "I'm afraid of what might happen. We can't get carried away."

"But Colette …"

His pleas were useless. They sat for a few more minutes in silence.

"I should take you back. It's late."

*   *   *   *

On September 3, Savino was busy all day, driving Captain DiLauro from the barracks to the mayor's house several times. The captain didn't speak at all while they were en route. Usually he was very talkative, sharing with Savino many details about his family. But today, the captain simply stared at the road in front of them, anxious to speak with his lieutenants at the barracks or to Colonel Modesto in the capital city of Ajaccio from the phone in the mayor's study.

In the evening, Savino was at the mayor's house yet again. Captain DiLauro and Mayor Poggi were in the study, where they had been for over an hour. Savino could hear their muffled conversation; some of it was very animated, but he was reluctant to get up from his seat to press his ear against the door. *If I'm caught, I'll be in trouble. It's better to stay seated; if I need to know what's going on, Captain DiLauro will tell me.* Savino couldn't imagine why the captain's demeanor had been so different all day.

Savino heard the door to the study open and lifted his head from the book he had taken from one of the mayor's shelves. He set it down when he noticed the concern on both men's faces.

"Captain, are you all right? Can I get you anything?"

"No. Take me to the barracks one last time and then back here."

On the way, Captain DiLauro told his driver what had been happening. "You'll know soon enough, so let me tell you. I'm about to ask the lieutenants to notify the troops about what has been happening. The British landed at Reggio Calabria today, and we've signed an armistice. No official announcement has been made, but it won't be long before Germany hears of it. We need to prepare for an attack."

"An attack by Germany? I don't understand. Germany is now our enemy?"

"Yes. And now that Corsica is in the Allies' hands, we can expect an invasion from Germany to regain it."

"France is now our ally?"

"Yes. I knew it would only be a matter of time since Mussolini fell in July. Apparently General Badoglio and King Victor Emmanuel have been negotiating a treaty ever since. Drive quickly."

As Savino drove, he thought of the battle that was sure to come and was frightened. He also realized that Colette was no longer considered the enemy. He wanted to tell her as soon as possible.

*　　　*　　　*　　　*

Savino waited impatiently as Captain DiLauro conferred with his lieutenants. He kept circling the car, kicking the ground, checking his watch every minute. It was past eight. He was hoping to get the captain back to Mayor Poggi's house before Colette retired for the night. They could drive to their spot, and Savino would tell her they were not enemies. Now she wouldn't be so fearful about showing her love.

At last, the captain came out of the officers' quarters and approached the staff car. Savino opened the door, helped the captain in, rushed to the driver's side, and started the engine. The tires kicked up gravel as he sped away.

"Easy, Private. The urgency is over for the moment."

Savino slowed the vehicle. "What happens now?"

"The French and Germans will be swarming over Corsica soon. We'll have to wait and see how determined Hitler is to keep this island."

Savino drove in silence to the mayor's house. Not knowing what their fate would be over the coming days, Savino was more determined than ever to be with Colette. It could possibly be their one and only time together.

After getting Captain DiLauro settled, Savino lingered for a few moments near the car. *Colette should have come out to see me by now*, he thought. She always knew when he was there; her room was near the stairs on the second floor, and she would have heard all the activity downstairs. It was a comfortable, pleasant night. Maybe she decided to get some fresh air and took a walk.

Savino walked toward the clearing where they always sat in the car. Once he found her, they could walk together, and he would explain how things had changed and how potentially dangerous the next few days and weeks might be.

He walked for fifteen minutes without finding Colette and saw no one else along the way. As he neared the clearing where he and Colette usually parked, he saw one of the other staff cars in the moonlight. A few soldiers had access to the cars when they weren't being used to take one of the officers somewhere. Who else would be out here?

Savino quietly approached the driver's side and looked in. Although the top was down, the occupants didn't hear him; they were too preoccupied with what they were doing. Savino almost turned away to leave the partially disrobed couple that was feverishly kissing, their faces obscured, hands roving over each other's bodies, passionately making love. Before he could back away, however, the woman's face came into view. It was Colette. Savino was stunned and inadvertently gasped, alerting the couple of his presence. As he stood there, Colette and the man she was with looked up in shock and quickly covered themselves. Savino then realized the man was Pietro.

At first, Savino stood motionless, in shock, as Colette and Pietro dressed.

"What are you doing here?" Pietro asked as he buttoned his shirt.

"What am *I* doing here?" Incredulous, Savino reached into the car, grabbed Pietro's shirt and pulled him out.

"What are you doing with Colette?" The veins in his neck bulging, Savino swung his fist at Pietro's face, but Pietro managed to evade the punch and grabbed Savino's arms. Savino freed himself and lunged at Pietro, bringing him to the ground.

The two soldiers wrestled, rolling around in the dirt, throwing punches that landed weakly at their targets. Savino managed to get Pietro face down and put his right arm around Pietro's neck, squeezing tightly. Pietro couldn't break the hold and banged on the ground with his right fist, coughing. Colette, watching from the car, saw Pietro's face turning red, his eyes bulging.

She jumped out of the car, screaming.

"Stop it! Would you both stop it? Now!"

Savino continued choking Pietro, ignoring Colette. She kicked Savino in his side and then pounded on his back with both fists.

"Savino, you're killing him. Stop! You're both behaving like animals. Stop fighting right now and get up!"

Slowly, Savino released his grip. After taking a few deep breaths to compose himself, he climbed off of Pietro and stood. Pietro rolled over and propped himself up on his elbows. Colette extended her hand to him and helped him up. The two men wiped the dirt from their clothes, warily eyeing each other.

Savino turned his attention to the woman he thought he loved. "Colette, how could you do this? We … we …"

"We what, Savino?" Colette was scolding him. "Do you think I belong to you?"

"I love you. I've told you a million times. How could you?"

Pietro walked over to lean on the car, still trying to catch his breath.

"You're a sweet boy, Savino," Colette said, easing up on her tone. "I like you. I enjoy spending a little time with you. But you're not a man yet. You've still got to grow up. I never said I loved you, did I? I never wanted to give you that impression."

"But I thought …"

"You think with your heart, Savino. Use your head. We're in the middle of a war. When this is over, you'll go home, and I'll stay here. We'll both be where we belong."

"And him?" Savino tilted his head in Pietro's direction. "He's the man you'd rather be with?" Pietro stood quietly, stuffing his shirttails into his pants, watching his former friend get a life lesson from Colette.

"What about him? His head isn't in the clouds, like yours. We're having fun. Enjoying each other for what we can give each other now. Not tomorrow. Not forever. Now."

"You don't love each other?"

Colette and Pietro stifled laughs, trying not to infuriate Savino.

"Savino, you fall in love too easily," Colette said, trying to defuse the situation. "Love isn't important now; especially now. Forget about falling in love."

"I don't understand how you could be this way. I thought you were virtuous. And you, Pietro. You knew how I felt. Why?"

"Savino, Colette told you. We're just having fun," Pietro said. "Nobody's in love here."

Savino shook his head. "Do what you want. Neither of you cared enough to think how you were betraying me. Have your fun. I won't bother either of you any more. You can both go to hell."

He turned, walked away, and never looked back.

The woman he loved had betrayed him. His closest friend had betrayed him. Even his country couldn't remain faithful to its cause, switching sides when it was more convenient. No one, and nothing, could be trusted.

Chapter 17
December 2003

*A*S BAD AS my relationship with my father had been throughout my life, it seemed to reach a new low after I learned that Leonard Klein had died. I couldn't begin to fathom how Dad seemingly took pleasure in Len's death simply because I had grown close to him.

Kathy convinced me to visit my father after I'd managed to avoid seeing him for nearly two weeks. I was still extremely angry, but she felt our prolonged absence would only make things worse for my mother.

As we entered the room, I noticed that Mr. O'Hara's nameplate was gone, and his bed was empty. Obviously, no one was sharing the room with my father at the moment. I had no idea whether Mr. O'Hara had died or was released, and I didn't bother asking. For all I knew, he may have requested to be moved to another room after witnessing our behavior a few weeks earlier.

My father had lost quite a bit of weight. He ate small amounts when a nurse fed him, even though he seemed capable of feeding himself. Because of this, he now had an I.V. tube to supplement his nutritional intake. As usual, his own stubborn behavior was making his situation worse.

His hair was now shorn close to the scalp, like a crew cut. I imagined the barber had done this for his own convenience.

Combined with his weight loss, he looked like a prisoner of war after a few years in the Hanoi Hilton.

My mother was there when Kathy and I arrived, sitting quietly, staring at him in the bed. His television was off, and the room was eerily silent. I leaned against the wall near my mother as Kathy went to the bed and planted a kiss on my father's forehead.

"How are you today, Dad?"

She got no response. He stared into space, ignoring her.

Kathy walked toward me, raising her eyebrows, her expression implying, "I tried." We remained silent for a few moments. Finally, I couldn't take it anymore.

"What's with him now?" I asked my mother, not caring that he would hear our conversation.

"I don't know. He hasn't said a word since I got here about an hour ago."

"You know," I said to my father, "you complain about us not visiting you enough, but if you're going to lie there like lox on a bagel when we're here, why should we bother?"

Kathy elbowed me in the ribs, so I decided to hold my tongue for my mother's sake. After a few more silent minutes, my mother asked about Lisa. It was good to talk about something positive. In anticipation of her spring graduation, Lisa had received an offer from the State Department for a position as a passport and visa specialist, which her student advisor had helped her obtain.

"Looks like all the money we gave to Princeton didn't go to waste," I said.

"She worked hard for it," Kathy added.

"Secretary of state can't be too far behind," I joked, glancing at my father, who had no reaction to Lisa's good luck.

Just then, an orderly carrying a tray of food entered the room. A heavyset nurse followed him in and walked toward my mother. I recognized her as Nancy Carlisle, the head nurse, whom I had seen on previous visits.

"Mrs. Giordano, if you have a moment, could you come out to the nurses' station?"

"Of course." My mother looked at me. "Tony, you come too, okay?"

As I walked out with my mother, she turned to Kathy. "If he doesn't feed himself, would you help him?"

"Sure, Mom."

As we approached the nurses' station, two other nurses rose to join us. I had seen them before, too, but didn't know their names. They were young, and I guessed they were novices or perhaps just a little more advanced. Nurse Carlisle said, "Let's all go in the nurses' lounge."

She closed the door behind us and motioned for us to sit at the table where the nurses ate their meals, hoping for a quiet moment away from the patients. Once we were settled, she said, "Mrs. Giordano, as you know, we've spoken several times since your husband was transferred from St. Luke's, primarily about his progress, or, more accurately, lack of progress."

"Yes, I know. He hasn't tried to help himself from the beginning."

"His stubbornness is just the start. I'm sorry to have to bring this up, but his attitude is worse than ever, and it's adversely affecting our staff. He's become very abusive." She nodded at the other two nurses and introduced us to Linda and Julia. The two young women had trouble looking directly at my mother and me. Linda's right leg was constantly moving as she rapidly bounced her heel up and down, and Julia tapped the fingers of both hands against the arm of her chair. Nancy Carlisle continued. "Yesterday, Linda went into the room to change his bed linens, and earlier in the day Julia took him for his bath. Linda, why don't you tell them what happened?"

"Well," Linda explained, putting her hands on her right knee, trying to stop her leg from twitching, "I was trying to help him to his feet to take him from the bed to the chair to sit while I made the bed. I grabbed him from under his arms to lift him. I know he's not so weak that he couldn't work with me to get up, but he wouldn't budge. He was like a dead weight. I asked him to work with me, but I guess that got him mad." Linda hesitated and looked at Nancy.

"Go ahead," said Nancy. "They need to know."

"Then he said, 'Get away from me, you … you.' He called me the c-word."

My mother put her hands to her mouth. "I am *so* sorry." My face flushed with anger.

Julia briefly told her story. "Basically the same thing happened to me when I went to get him for his bath. He wouldn't let me get him out of the bed and called me the same thing. He never got his bath."

"I'll talk to him," I said, ashamed. "There's no excuse for that kind of behavior."

"Whatever you tell him," Nancy said, "will reinforce what I told him earlier today. I said we'd transfer him out of here if he didn't apologize. He didn't even make eye contact with me when I spoke to him. I'm sure he realizes we're discussing him right now."

"That would explain the silent treatment we're getting," I said. "He knows he's wrong but will never admit it."

We all rose. "I'm sorry. I'll make sure nothing like this happens again," I told the nurses as we left the lounge.

My mother and I got back to my father's room in time to see Kathy moving the tray table away from the bed and straightening up. She appeared flustered.

"Did he eat anything?" my mother asked.

"Not much." Kathy concentrated on what she was doing, replacing the cover on the dish and cleaning the table, not looking at us.

I walked over to the bed and looked at my father for a few seconds. His steely eyes stared at me, challenging me to say what he knew was coming.

"Why do you continue to be such a bastard to everyone—even the nurses who are just trying to help you? They're doing their jobs, and you have to insult them using the most degrading word you can think of. You're an embarrassment to all of us."

He continued to stare, not caring what I was saying.

"The head nurse said she told you she'd have you transferred if you don't start respecting the people around here. Is that what you want? To go to a different place so you can abuse some new people?

If that happens, none of us will bother with you. You can stay there and rot for all I care."

"Tony, that's enough." My mother took me by the arm. "He understands."

"Apologize to those nurses the next time you see them." I turned to Kathy. "It's getting late. We should go. Ma, are you staying?"

"A little longer. I want to talk to your father."

"Let's go, Kathy. I'll see you, Ma."

We left the room, leaving my mother alone with him. I didn't know why she wanted to stay. There was nothing else she could have told him. If he didn't have enough sense to apologize after what I said and what Nancy Carlisle had told him earlier, nothing she said to him could make a difference.

*   *   *   *

Kathy and I drove home mostly in silence. I started a few conversations, but she was distant the whole time. As we pulled into the driveway, Kathy looked all around her seat and then turned to glance in the back of the car.

"I don't believe it," she said. "I forgot my purse in your father's room."

"That's not like you," I said. "You're always so organized."

"I'm pretty sure I know what happened." She took a deep breath. "I need to tell you something."

"You look upset. What's wrong? What happened?"

"When you and your mother left with that nurse, your mother asked me to feed your father if he didn't feed himself."

"Right. You were cleaning up when we got back. I'm sure you had to feed him."

"Yes, but ..." She was having a difficult time telling me what happened. I waited until she was ready to continue.

"I gave him a few mouthfuls. It was just meatloaf and mashed potatoes. He didn't say a word, but I guessed he didn't want any more. I told him he had to eat some more to keep up his strength. It was like talking to a child. Anyway, I managed to get some more into his mouth. He didn't try to swallow it. He just looked right at me and spit it out in my face. I guess I was rattled and just in a hurry to leave when you got back."

"That fucking bastard!" I thought for a moment. "If you hadn't forgotten your purse, you wouldn't have told me, would you?"

"I don't know. There's enough friction with everyone already." She paused. "Don't go back for it now. It can wait."

"No, it can't. Your wallet, license, keys. You'll need that stuff in the morning. I'll go back."

"Okay, but promise you won't say anything."

"He spit in your face, for Christ's sake."

"Please. Not tonight. You're upset."

"All right. I promise. I'll just go in, grab your purse, and leave." I opened the garage door with the remote so she could get into the house through the garage. "Go in the house. I won't be long."

Driving back, I debated whether I should keep my word. It wasn't like he had some kind of dementia and didn't know what he was doing. His behavior with the nurses was bad enough, but he spit in Kathy's face. I had to say something. But I had promised. Kathy and I have always been honest with each other. If she found out I said something to him, she'd be more upset with me than with him. I decided to go in and out, just like I'd said I would.

I hoped my father would be asleep when I arrived so he'd never know I was there, but he was awake, watching television. I looked around for the purse and quickly saw it on the windowsill. As I walked over to get it, he said, "What … are you … doing here?"

"Are those your first words of the day? Kathy forgot her purse. It's over there." I pointed to the windowsill.

"Son … come here … first."

Now he wants to talk? I thought. The "son" grated at me as usual. After what we'd gone through earlier, I couldn't believe he was making an attempt at civility. I walked to the side of the bed and looked down at him. The head of his bed was angled up a little.

"What? I just want to get the purse and go home."

"You hate me … don't you?"

"Dad, not now. I really have to go." The old man looked weaker than he had when I saw him earlier, or maybe he was just tired.

"Was I … a good father … at all?"

"What?" I snapped. "Were you a good father? What do you think? You've been totally worthless as a father and a husband. You made our lives miserable. But I won't let you abuse my wife." I spit in his face. "That's for Kathy."

Enraged, I reached for one of the spare pillows lying at his side and with the other hand pulled out his nasal cannula. I pressed the pillow down on his face, wiping my saliva off in the process. His hands weakly grasped my arms, and I could see his legs moving slowly under the sheets as he struggled uselessly to fight back. I continued to press down and heard a muffled sound come through the pillow. Did he say *connect*? *Correct*? *Collect*? I couldn't make it out. He wasn't making any sense. I pressed harder and noticed that his feet had stopped moving.

Suddenly, I came to my senses. *What am I doing?* I threw the pillow on the bed and replaced the cannula. His eyes were wide open, but he was motionless. *Did I stop in time?*

Within seconds, I knew the answer. The monitor buzzed, displaying a flat line. I tried not to panic. He was very sick and getting worse. This would have happened soon anyway, I rationalized. After glancing around the room to make sure nothing looked suspicious, I ran out to get a nurse and to call my mother.

Chapter 18
The Cittern

*A*BOUT TWO WEEKS after the funeral, my mother asked me to help her go through some of my father's things. His den included two filing cabinets and a desk whose drawers were stuffed with years of receipts, bank and brokerage statements, tax returns going back decades, and other items that were no longer of any importance. In addition, she wanted me to help her clear out his closet and dresser to make a clothing donation to some local charities. Anything unusable would be thrown away. It was a job I knew would take me several weekends to complete. Although I felt it was an imposition on my time, I approached the task as a way to finally rid myself, and my mother, of any remnants of my father.

I arrived at the house early the first Saturday after New Year's Day and walked into the den. My father's refuge had become a dumping ground for everything. In addition to the various documents I expected to find, numerous books and periodicals littered the top of his desk and the floor surrounding it. I had to step over several piles just to be able to sit in his old chair.

"Ma, this place is a disaster area. Don't you ever throw anything out?"

"I know I'm bad, but your father was worse. He wouldn't let me touch anything in here. I couldn't even clean—I couldn't find the floor to vacuum."

"Well, this is going to be a bigger job than I thought. Do you trust me to throw out what I don't think is important?"

"Do whatever you think is best."

"Okay. Why don't you go and do whatever you would be doing now. I'll start by separating this stuff into keep and discard piles. I have a feeling most things will be in the discard pile."

"I need some things at the supermarket. I'll leave you alone."

After she left, I sat a few minutes, surveying every inch of the room and wondering where I should begin. My first instinct was to get a few boxes of large trash bags and get rid of everything, but I decided to do the job right. There might be something worthwhile in this load of crap. I started with the floor, since I could simply shift things into their appropriate pile. I methodically looked at every item. *Time* magazines that had been saved for no obvious reason were stacked in one corner. A few had covers that I felt were of some historical significance, so I put them in the keep pile.

I crawled from item to item, and my gaze fell on the small curio cabinet in one corner. It was partially hidden by one of the filing cabinets, and I hadn't noticed it at first. It had quietly guarded its contents for over forty years. My childhood curiosity and stubbornness were why my father had bought it. I couldn't help thinking that if my father had spent as much time caring for his family as he did protecting the cittern, we'd all have been much better off. I stood up, walked toward it, and stared inside for a few minutes. I hadn't appreciated what a beautiful instrument the cittern was when I was younger, but now I could see what had attracted my father to it.

No one would stop me this time. I reached for the handle to open the cabinet. It was locked. No one who would have touched it had been in the house for years. I wondered if he'd been afraid of it being abused all this time, or if perhaps he hadn't picked it up himself for a long while. I had to open the cabinet. I went to his desk and rummaged through the drawers. I briefly picked up and flipped through his old telephone directory, remembering a time years ago when I'd watched him do the same thing, one of the few times I'd felt he loved me.

It didn't take a lot of searching before I found an old prescription bottle holding a single key in the middle drawer. I walked to the cabinet and tried it. The door opened. Reaching in, I carefully removed the cittern and held it straight out, really admiring it for the first time. It was a beautiful instrument, with an almond-shaped body and a slightly rounded back. The luster of the finish was still very evident. There was something feminine about the way it looked and felt. It had five pairs of strings, which I thought would have made it difficult to learn to play, although I remembered my father getting some decent sounds out of it.

I had never displayed any musical talent, but I decided to sit down and see what I could do. I knew it would be considered an antique and wondered if there was a market for it.

As I sat down, I swung the cittern around to place it on my lap as I had seen my father do. When I moved it, I heard a clicking sound and felt something shift inside the instrument. Outwardly nothing seemed wrong, but I shook it slightly and heard the noise again. Something was inside the cittern. Turning it horizontally with the sound hole facing down, I held it over my head and kept shaking. I could sense whatever was inside moving closer to the hole. Soon, what looked like heavy paper came into view. Tilting the cittern, I managed to get the paper to come through the hole and rest on the strings. Holding the cittern level with my left hand, I moved the paper to get it to come completely out and then tapped on it to dislodge it from the strings.

The paper fell onto the desk. I put the cittern aside and picked up the paper. Two pieces of dried-out cellophane tape were on either side of it. Years ago, my father must have removed the strings, taped the paper inside, and then restrung the cittern. I didn't think he would have gone through that trouble without a good reason.

The paper was folded in half, and as I picked it up and unfolded it, I realized there were two pieces of paper, which turned out to be old, creased, black-and-white photographs. The first showed a young boy, about eight years old, with a mangy-looking dog.

I turned it over and saw an inscription in what I thought was a woman's handwriting: *Savino e Rigoletto —1930.* Turning back to the photograph, I stared at the boy. I couldn't believe that was my father. He was a pretty cute kid. He had a huge smile and was kneeling in front of a tree next to the dog, with his arms around the dog's neck. He hated dogs and had never allowed me to have one, but here he was, obviously with a beloved pet.

The second photograph raised even more questions. It was a young lady, maybe twenty years old, standing in front of what looked like a large wooden church door. It definitely wasn't my mother, because I had seen plenty of old family photographs over the years and would have recognized her. Turning it over, I saw another inscription. This one appeared to be in my father's handwriting, although a younger, steadier version of it: *Colette Poggi, Corsica —1943.*

I couldn't help noticing how beautiful she was. But who was she? Nineteen forty-three was a war year. I knew my father had served in the Italian army during World War II, but he'd never talked about it. I had no idea where he'd been stationed, but it was obvious that he'd been in Corsica at some point in his life. I couldn't even be sure this photograph had anything to do with the war.

I put the photographs side by side on the desk, looking from one to the other. *What were the stories behind these pictures?* Dad had kept so many things inside, and these two photographs were clearly very important to him. At least now I had a little better idea of why he never wanted anyone touching his precious instrument. Maybe if things had been different, if he had sought help for his anxiety, if I had been less rebellious and tried to see things from his perspective, I would have known more.

I suddenly remembered Dad's last day at Tranquil Meadows, although I wanted to forget those horrible last minutes with him. The sounds he was making through the pillow. He wasn't saying *"Connect"* or *"Collect."* His last words, his last thought, concerned Colette. It now made sense. But what did she mean to him?

Suddenly I had many questions that would remain unanswered. There were so many lost opportunities to have a better relationship, now gone forever. The finality of it hit me at once. I started crying for him; crying for all of us, Anna, my mother, and myself.

I found a box of tissues on his desk and reached for a few. Drying my eyes, I stared at the photograph of Colette. She was looking straight at me, and she was smiling.